# Kaya
# Days

# Kaya
# Days

CARL DE SOUZA

TRANSLATED FROM FRENCH BY
**JEFFREY ZUCKERMAN**

TWO LINES
PRESS

Originally published as *Les Jours Kaya*
© 2000 by Editions de l'Olivier
Translation © 2021 by Jeffrey Zuckerman

Two Lines Press
582 Market Street, Suite 700, San Francisco, CA 94104
www.twolinespress.com

ISBN: 978-1-949641-19-6
Ebook ISBN: 978-1-949641-20-2

Cover design by Gabriele Wilson
Cover photo © Lexi Laine / Millennium Images, UK
Design by Sloane | Samuel

Library of Congress Cataloging-in-Publication Data:
Names: Souza, Carl de, 1948- author.
Zuckerman, Jeffrey, 1987- translator.
Title: Kaya days / Carl de Souza ; translated by Jeffrey Zuckerman.
Other titles: Jours Kaya. English
Description: San Francisco, CA : Two Lines Press, [2021]
Originally published as Les Jours Kaya.
Identifiers: LCCN 2021015291 (print) | LCCN 2021015292
(ebook) | ISBN 9781949641202 (ebook) | ISBN 9781949641196
(trade paperback)
Classification: LCC PQ3989.2.S674 (ebook) | LCC PQ3989.2.S674
J6813 2021 (print) | DDC 843/.914--dc23
LC record available at https://lccn.loc.gov/2021015291

1 3 5 7 9 10 8 6 4 2

To Pramesh

Santee always liked the bloody, ruddy reds. So Ram would pick the blacks, saying the dark offset the nickel-plated kogs even more. She and Ram would count them off as they parked, decked out by the families in garlands and balloons for a wedding, or as they started and stopped in campaign parades, flags tied to the rear dafs. Santee was pouting: she wouldn't be debating with Ram today, they wouldn't be sparring with words that Ma didn't understand, with their own terms for blinkers and hubcaps. She was too old for all that, she knew, but if Ram had waited for her today, they could have played reds against blacks—she would have insisted, she would have begged until he relented, and would have won outright, and only then would they have gone back home on the last bus and Ma wouldn't have asked any questions. The disappointment of this loss was far worse than any distress she felt at Ram being no-where to be found.

The shadows grew chilly along the low wall on which she was sitting, among the boys her little brother's age, and Santee knew he was al-ready gone. Nobody had said those words, but she knew, maybe she'd known even before coming to Rose-Hill. She wasn't sure what exactly she was waiting for as she watched the parents in their cars picking up their sons. The boys' dark uni-forms were a stark contrast to her pink taffeta dress, her too-long limbs, and her braids gleam-ing with coconut oil. One of them had scoffed as she'd wavered in the doorway. The teacher had given her an earful and then, after checking a list, shrugged. Bissoonlall? Ram Bissoonlall? He's left already. Everyone glared at her as if it was her fault. It was, she knew; she ought to have moved faster, come earlier, hurried like the boys rushing down the street, the parents who found their sons and sped off in their red cars. But Santee hadn't been able to come earlier. When Ma had told her to pick up Ram, she'd been puzzled, wondering why Ma was asking her to go when she herself, despite being old, liked doing it. Something must have been off, or the tides were all wrong, Don't you ever go against the tides was what Ma told Santee when she was thirteen and had come to her mother convinced that her stomach was ripping open. Ma had been trying to warn her of the dangers in store for her as a girl.

Getting dressed had taken her more than an hour with some scolding, but not too much. Something was definitely wrong; any other day Ma would have reminded her sternly of her responsibilities as the older child. Santee let the first few buses at the Bienvenue stop go past; by the time she was on the next one, she wasn't thinking about Ram anymore. The countryside was rolling by faster than all the other times she'd gone to Rose-Hill with Ma—little hills prickling with traveler's palms, pale fields, sun-bleached temples. Nobody was headed into town; everybody was going home. In the huge bus careering upward, the empty seats rattled and there was only her, the driver with his hands swinging this way and that, and a long-haired, badly shaven conductor who stumbled down the aisle, his young face leering as he told her just how dangerous it was for a young girl to be traveling alone. She didn't respond, just twisted her little hanky between her fingers and stared out at the sugarcane fields as the jeer blew past the nape of her neck like so much hot air.

As long as cars kept coming she could keep on sitting on the low wall, as long as the stream was steady, dotted by reds like a pulse, she felt a sense of safety, even if she knew it was short-lived. For now, she didn't have to watch the teacher dealing with the other boys, didn't have to go from classroom to classroom only to hear his shouted name—Bissoonlall!—echoing in the empty rooms. Nobody would bother her as she took in this place Ram had the privilege to experience every day. For now, she could make sense of the scraps of the stories he parceled out when Ma interrogated him at dinner, paltry crumbs that now connected to something real, amid the foliage of the school's grounds, the motors' revving, the boys' taunts.

As long as the cars went by, she wouldn't have to deal with the prospect of going back to Bienvenue without Ram, in a rush like everyone else, but for no clear reason. She was relishing those last few moments of stillness, the stone harsh against her skin. She let its chill seep through the fabric of her dress and across her lower body, knowing that any minute now everything would force her, just like the others, to go straight home. Ram hadn't waited for her.

But all this had happened gradually, with the quiet of a new beginning. She recalled the small shock she'd felt at Ma's words, Go pick up Ram, and she remembered the particular weariness in Ma's voice, how she seemed to withdraw in some way with those clipped words. Ma entrusted her with this responsibility, not because she trusted her daughter, but because she had no strength left. Santee didn't hold it against her. What did Ma do after she left? She must have wrapped her odhni around her head, despite the heat, and gone into her bedroom. And then she'd have gone to sleep, even though Ma was never in bed during the day.

The cars took away the last of the children and their chatter. The wind blew a wad of paper across the long stretch of asphalt with some rustling, and a few voices, the last ones, overlapped, mingled: I told you to check the classrooms, chief, can't be leaving any of the kids behind, The Sacré Cœur's on fire, haven't you heard? Santee stood up.

She followed a lady and her son heading down the street by the church toward Trèfles. The teacher locked up behind them. Santee watched the hand clutching the boy's. At that age, there's no holding their hand—they wander off, they kick pebbles as far as they can. Santee wondered if Ma would have taken Ram's hand like that as they went to the Rose-Hill station; was that why he hadn't waited? She remembered how damp Ram's palms always were and how, when he was younger, everyone always insisted he'd been playing in the water and told him he'd catch a cold that way. The boy and his mother were talking in whispers, aimlessly; she must have hurried from work after the announcement had come on the radio to go pick up children from school, and she was taking him—her love, her life—home without paying any attention to the people standing in the doorways or the sirens blaring in the town center. Santee couldn't recall ever having had her hand grabbed like that; she wasn't wistful, but it had to feel odd to have your hand clutched in a woman's thick fingers, to sense her sturdy frame beside yours. Santee's eyes rested on the massive rear rolling like a gentle sea, and she let herself be led past the banks of wooden houses. Men charged past them every so often. Snippets of small talk, bits of jokes and snickers. The sharp air stung as they forged ahead, toward the muffled explosions she could almost feel in her bones. She needed to stay in the lady's wake, with Ram's town all around her, sheltering her; he had to be here, she was sure of it, but where exactly? He'd been so unwilling to share this world with them, and now she knew it was because they would have floundered here, Ma being as weary as Santee was naïve. At Hugnin Road, the lady barely slowed down and crossed without looking either way for trucks: the boy's hand in hers was her carte blanche. The traffic signals on both sides lay toppled, and acrid fumes wafted from burning tires. The lady shoved her way through a gaggle of men swigging bottles of beer outside a laboutik sinwa. Santee slipped through the gap. The men closed in behind them, shielding them from the explosions. They emerged onto a narrow side street in Trèfles. The mother, the son, and Santee—nobody else. Their footsteps resounded beneath the mango trees arching be-tween the rows of houses. The lady kept looking back and glaring at her. But Santee wouldn't be shaken off; she knew this wasn't a place where she could afford to assume anything. She would rather let them take the lead. The mother and the boy came to a cast-iron gate shaped like a scallop and painted blue. She took out a key, opened it, and made her kid go in first. Santee heard him say: That's Bissoonlall's sister. The lady practically shoved the boy into a small garden with flower-pots and a birdcage. She stood by the gate until Santee disappeared down the alleyway.

Santee didn't dare go back to ask the boy if he knew where Ram was. She could see the lights switching on in the ground-floor windows, then hands yanking the curtains shut. Bissoonlall's out...Bissoonlall's always out...Bissoonlall finn al kazino... Those whispers were her only hope of bringing him back home. It was getting dark under the mango trees. She had no hope of un-derstanding, but that wasn't what she needed to do, that wasn't her job, she was just here because Ma couldn't be. What she needed to do was find Ram; one of these alleys would lead to him, but which one?

Santee had never been methodical when looking for Ram back in Bienvenue. She'd always run out into the street first, then gone behind the house and kept going all the way down to the river, yelling his name over and over as her hopes flagged. Those minutes, as Ram's name hung over the house, were always terrifying. They stretched out. He always chose the perfect moment to end her torment, usually when the kitchen door opened and Ma added her voice to the chorus, tired of hearing Santee yelling all around the house. But here in Trèfles, where Creoles were living practically on top of one another, Santee couldn't launch Ramesh's name into the air, couldn't send her anxious, Hindu intonation soaring.

Raaaa-messshhhh.

It was the sort of name that forged onward alone, breaking like a wave on the shore, across the tangled alleyways. She wouldn't have had to repeat it. What she needed to do now was walk randomly amid the indistinguishable intersections, since she no longer had Corps de Garde mountain, the rocky face of which the woman and the child had more or less disappeared into, to orient her. When she decided to go back to talk

13

to the boy, there was no seashell-shaped gate to be found. The road stretched out beneath a deepening night. Under a streetlight, men were talking over one another: They beat him, I'm telling you he had gone stone-cold turkey, No they punched his mouth in, Nobody saw it, They left him to die, Bullshit, ase koz kaka, they've done it to others, he's not the first Creole to die in prison. Nobody looked twice at her. She didn't dare ask them where the casino was; she would rather have found a woman to ask. Music floated from a store's verandah, music and the voices of a few teenagers trying to stay in the shadows. The reddish glow of their joints was all she could make out. It was clear none of them had been talking, not for a good while. They had been smoking, smoking and singing snippets of a dirge that unfurled with the men's bass tones, the women's reedy voices. Santee got closer to make out their faces, but among the mass of dreadlocked heads nothing stood out. She aimed her question at an especially shrill voice in the corner. All she could see were the whites of eyes. Where do I find the casino? The song died, but no one paid attention to the newcomer, her question lingered, bothersome, nobody cared. The beer bottles were passed around, clinking, a ravanne's beat continued past the song's end. The casino? Nobody on the store's verandah looked surprised, nothing seemed to reach them, the sound of the ravanne rose up and drew them back in. There's a gambling house down Prince of Wales Street, but it might be closed? The girl pointed down the road and they picked up the song where they'd left off, the music even more insistent now. Santee set out. The girl had said to count off five streets. She shouldn't make any mistakes this time, she had no excuse, each intersection was brightly lit. But when she paused at the second one, she realized the night was nipping at her heels, the soundless night—a darkness blacking out each intersection. Two men were following her. Two? She could hear their voices, calm yet implacable, voices that kept pace with her, their tone shifting as a rock was thrown at a streetlight bulb. They hit the mark each time. Santee started running to stay in the light. From the houses, she could hear televisions blaring the weather report. The characteristics of a slight high-pressure system over the Mascarenes, droned a reporter; Santee decided that was the explanation for the distant explosions she heard in Ram's world—it was just the storm, even though these were nothing like the thunderclaps off Mulâtresse mountain in Bienvenue. The tree-tops were dark against a reddish blaze. Lightning bolts could be tinged that color, she thought, it's electricity in the air, when we're in Ram's world that's what it has to be. She could make out a rather busy main road ahead. The casino can't be far off now. Police vans with flashing lights sped by every so often. A cab pulled in ahead of her with a squeal of the tires and stopped in front of a building. It let out two Chinese women who kept chatting with the driver. Santee headed toward them to ask which way the casino was. The cab drove off. The Chinese women were still talking, but Santee didn't understand what they were saying. They had to be workers from one of the textile factories. They could talk all they liked, but she was only thinking about one thing: finding Ram. She asked them, very slowly, if they knew a boy by that name: I'm his sister, I'm from far away, I have to find him because... Their expressions turned serious, there was a quick back-and-forth, and then the two women each took one of her arms solemnly and escorted her into the building. A flashing sign indicated that they were walking into the Négus Pool House Night

Club. A row of bare lightbulbs cast a yellow glare
along the wall leading inside and zigged up a
level. In the stairwell, a shabbily suited man's
slurred goodbyes echoed loudly. He clung drunk-
enly to the banister, slumped over it so they could
get by him and head upstairs. A tall, elegant
Taiwanese woman in a turquoise-striped dress
stood next to him. There was a brief discussion
between her and the two women, then they continued up to a cavernous room with Santee in
tow. A billiard table covered by a tarp stood im-
posingly in the center. Along the walls, slot machines and electronic games jingled and squealed,
distracting from the lack of customers. Santee
saw, behind a bar covered with fake flowers across
from the entrance, a young guy in a military shirt
and sunglasses. Good evening, Shyam! the two
Chinese women shouted. An elbow on the bar
propped up his tilted head as he smiled curtly. His
lips lazily formed words, and the tremors ran
across the rest of his body, but Santee couldn't
hear him or even the music over the machines'
din. Above the bar, the plaster bust of a bearded
man with high cheekbones bore the same knowing smile. It reassured Santee to come in from the
night and see smiles. The welcoming presence of

the bearded man, no doubt a Christian saint, set her at ease. Shyam had festooned him in the Hindu style so that HAILE was the only part of his nameplate she could see. The unexpected gleam and babble of the machines charmed Santee—all of this was just like Ram, who was always being given extravagant yet flimsy toys that the two of them tinkered with together. Santee began to smile as well. The guy at the bar pulled his hand away from his cheek, revealing the cell phone he had been whispering into, stood upright, and called out to the two women. They rushed over to tell him something—they must have been explaining that Santee was just passing through, that she didn't want to be a bother, and that she was just Ram's sister. The guy put down his phone and fixed his eyes on her. The two women waited. Then Shyam shrugged: So that's Ram's sister, huh? He lost interest in the women, turning back to his phone with his enigmatic smile, and Santee was allowed to follow the women into a rear corridor. They stepped out onto a balcony abutting that of an old wood building. There were the smells of a kitchen. An infant's cries rose over the electronics. A woman's firm, sweet voice tried to soothe the baby. To their left ran a series of rooms; from one of them came the clink of dominoes. The women slipped into the next one. There was a row of disused urinals co-cooned in green-polka-dotted covers, and, along a wall, metal desks dragged in from some office that had oval mirrors with carved wooden frames propped up on them. The same fake flowers were everywhere. None of it was dusty; someone kept the room squeaky clean. There was even a fan and a radio playing music, as well as two Formica-paneled armoires and a couch made out of old car seats where a Creole woman slept, her head thrown back, an arm shielding her eyes from the light. Her dress had slid up, revealing pink pant-ies, and her bare legs swung back and forth. The two Chinese women pulled clothes out of the ar-moire, took off their jeans and T-shirts, and put on identical, striped dresses. The two were very different heights: one was willowy while the other was rather short and plump. Santee saw that, oddly enough, the dresses suited them both. She stood by the doorway and watched them both put on makeup. They had taken quite a few small con-tainers out of the drawers beneath the counters, and now slathered large brown splotches of foun-dation on their cheeks, caked mascara on their eyelashes, and made crimson fruits out of their lips. The chubby one's eyes paused when they met Santee's in the mirror. She then went back to making herself up, intent, checking Santee's reaction to see whether she approved. After a few casual pencil strokes, the tall one was done and headed back to the main room. The other one nodded Santee over; she sat down in front of the mirror. The girl didn't dare to touch the makeup. She looked at her own face, at the too-thick eyebrows, the long lashes she batted anxiously as she stared at her light brown irises; it was all so unlike the smooth, perfectly done Chinese woman's. The woman, too, was scrutinizing her chestnut skin gleaming under the lights with the sweat of having walked all the way across Trèfles, then she ran her finger across Santee's damp forehead, leaving behind a matte streak. She began to wipe Santee's temples dry with toilet paper, then untied the black velvet bow and let her hair free. Its thickness was surprising. She hesitated before trying to tame the mane and the girl's unruly features. Santee waited patiently, her hands folded over her knees. Li Chen! the other woman yelled from the billiard room. Li Chen barked a reply as she began knotting Santee's hair into a heavy chignon. Then she set to powdering her skin.

Santee saw a new face materialize: pale white, almost as light as Li Chen's. It floated atop her long brown neck in the bathroom's dimness. Santee felt the thick layer of foundation straining the skin of her cheekbones and she tasted the lipstick. The labor was broken up by Li Chen's satisfied chuckling and incomprehensible scolding. Li Chen had her stand up as she stepped back to admire her handiwork. She moved right back in and pursed her lips at Santee's pink taffeta dress. Li Chen was right. There was no use in transforming her face only for Ram to see her in the same old dress. Li Chen began unbuttoning it. Santee helped her and watched as her clothes fell piece by piece to the ground. She saw her dark body emerging from that pink taffeta dress, her arms slowly unfurling, her torso stretching for her breasts to bloom. They rested on her slightly protruding ribcage, she pulled her shoulders up the better to support them. Behind that dark young woman with heavy breasts and a white mask in the mirror, Santee saw Li Chen rush to the armoire. Santee didn't hear any of the Chinese woman's muttering; all she saw were her lips fluttering, and she waited for her to talk to the tall girl with a

body like a palm tree. Li Chen came right back
with a garnet dress and alarmingly high heels.
Faster, Ram here soon. Santee saw the guy from
the bar silhouetted in the doorway and yelled. Li
Chen ran to shut the door. Curses rang out from
the other side as Li Chen urged Santee to hurry.
Shyam had been saying she'd be wise not to keep
Ram waiting. Santee didn't have any time to take
in her new look; she had to trust Li Chen, who
was already dragging her back into the billiard
room. The baby had stopped crying and the only
noise was from a television Shyam had turned
on. Two men were at the bar talking to Shyam
as the women arrived. The Chinese women were
getting ready to leave with them. Stay here,
Shyam told Santee, Ram's coming soon. Then,
disappointedly, to the men: She's Ram's sister.
They digested this detail and left the room. Li
Chen took one last look at Santee and walked off
after the men.

I wonder how Ram got it in his head to tell
you to come here. Santee rushed to explain: He's
always had a mind of his own. This seemed to sat-
isfy Shyam, who turned his attention back to the
TV. After the rebroadcast of the weather was a
report on the crisis in Kosovo. Santee took a seat

on a barstool, unsurprised that Ram commanded respect here. In the village, at Ma's, Ram was the center of the universe. Even when he was a newborn, back when Santee was five, everybody had crowded around his cradle. Pa, who was still alive then, had taken Santee in his arms so she could watch Ma breastfeed Ram. That's your little brother, Santee, take good care of him, help your mommy look after him. It wasn't hard to look after Ram, it was nothing at all; he was gifted and his babble quickly turned to words that everybody discussed at family get-togethers, convinced he had a bright future. They kept saying he got the knack of things faster than anyone else, without even trying. When Pa died, Ma started working at the sweater factory to pay for Ram's school, and so Santee finished primary school only to replace Ma at home. She, too, was convinced Ram was a genius, and the hours each day before Ram came home from school were lifeless.

There was a commotion at the bottom of the stairs; Santee could pick out the whine of a diesel engine, it must be a big car, maybe an Albion, and some voices. It's Ram. Shyam got up and ran down the stairs, only to come right back up, yelling to Santee: Gogot! Goddamn it! Ram's dead!

Santee stayed, motionless on her stool. Creole men were pouring into the room, pushing aside chairs and tables. The younger ones walked in backward, carrying a man's body. She could tell from their unsteadiness that he was fairly heavy, but she couldn't see him well amid the scrum. There was some rapid-fire bickering with Shyam, and then the men heaved the body onto the billiard table as Shyam turned on the light above it. The man's face was peaceful, with a chinstrap beard and thick lips covering a toothless jaw. She could see a bit of the whites of his eyes and his breaths came in muted growls. What she had taken for a pillow was in fact his mess of hair stuffed into a wool hat. She was surprised by the strange color of his shirt, and then realized, upon seeing a small puddle on the plastic tarp, that it was drenched in blood. Someone was saying he should go straight to the hospital, but Shyam rejected that idiotic idea with an onslaught of profanity, followed by more curses for having dragged this corpse-to-be here. The men kept their mouths shut and their heads bowed: they knew what Shyam was risking if the man was found here. His voice kept rising as he paced and waved his hands in disbelief, but he hadn't looked at the dying man. He finally took a breath and fixed his eyes on him.

You kouyon son of a bitch.

Tell me you're happy now, go on, say it. You baise-ou-maman Creole pilon, spitting up blood, dying on me? Look at this pile of bez you got me in... Who here's gonna bury your puant corpse now? Didn't nobody tell you all Creoles are good for is fann kaka? For once me and you finally got our bez done with, everything nice and easy, but this Black man here still ain't kontan? Has to go and sit his fess on a hundred red ants! Anybody bent on getting hisself killed, be my guest! How many times I got to say it? Don't you get no ideas, you're nothing more than a kou Creole, that's what you are! We're finally getting some tourists in here, there was some guy from Réunion yesterday, but now you, you...

What the guy bleeding to death had done was so serious that Shyam had run out of swears. One of the men who'd carried him in started yelling back, got louder, threatened to kill Shyam if he didn't stop shit-talking Creoles, but some of the other men stepped in and pulled him away. Santee heard their footsteps going downstairs, heard more expletives followed by pleas to calm down, then it all faded away.

Now Shyam had finally found a few more choice words. At some point, he had to stop to catch his breath. His eyes ran over the billiard room defiled by this bloody body. The machines gleamed and screeched louder and louder, as if there were only a few more minutes until some horrific tragedy, as if they were begging Shyam for protection, as if he understood, as if he could do something. Santee glimpsed Shyam's eyes tearing up behind his sunglasses, he waved affectionately, impotently, at the slot machines. There was nothing to be done at moments like this. He stepped back, took in the bar, the bottles of whiskey, the statue, the fan. And then he aimed his words at Santee:

Your brother is the worst liki sorma that ever lived.

He let that sink in. He could have been working here like me, but he's been out in the streets. Getting himself into all sorts of lamerdma like it's pussy. Santee nodded: Yes, Ram would have done better to be here than to leave Shyam high and dry. But Shyam was really getting carried away. The machines might be able to be saved, he just had to tell the police that this man had been brought in by his friends, that Shyam had nothing to do with it, that it was all just a misunderstanding.

Look at this! He leaned over to let her get an eyeful of his outfit. Santee thought he looked quite elegant in his leopard-print suit. I've got it nice here... This spot really is something, you know. Just guess how much kas I been offered for the Négus. Go on, name a number...

Santee had no idea, it had to be a lot. Shyam wasn't wrong, she really did like the twinkling of the machines, the heaps of fake flowers. The Négus was the kind of place that made everyone who came in smile, and all Li Chen's efforts had her feeling beautiful here in Shyam's casino. He had made a good life for himself; there was no point trawling the streets if you had a place like this. An explosion even louder than the others shook the walls and Santee could see a fire through the curtains. And now what am I gonna do with your body, Ram? Listen. You think I want to let you rot here? On my nice billiard table? The prone man groaned. Your friends cleared out, any second now they'll be getting in bagar with the police. Setting the whole town on fire, and I'm stuck here with you. Kaka liki. Shyam's voice cracked in a sob. He dragged his stool over and muttered things she couldn't hear to the figure lying there. She could tell they weren't sweet nothings, and decided that what Shyam was confiding to the Creole man was between the two of them, and that she ought to go find her little brother—but where? She tried to walk quietly, but her high heels clacked on the floorboards. Where are you going? Santee wasn't sure what to tell him. Now you're fucking off, too? You see me in this bez and all you can think is to run, you pitin? You're exactly like your kouyonad brother, you filthy pitin. A lump rose in Santee's throat as she stammered that she didn't mean to leave him all alone with a dying man but she abso-lutely had to find her brother Ram, and she would come back right away, no question. With Ram, of course, if Shyam would just be patient. Shyam got up and grabbed her wrist. His tears had traced long, salty streaks down his cheeks from under his sunglasses. Rambo's right here and he's dead. Fini. Sek. Don't you understand? There's no other Ram, the only one I know is this one, your brother an kouyonad Rambo who's dead and now there's just you and me. Help me, I'm begging you, help me. His other hand was in Santee's hair, undoing

her chignon. He pressed his face to her belly and
started bawling: Ram's dead. Santee tried to pull
away but Shyam's hand clutched her wrist even
tighter. She started struggling; she didn't try to
yell, maybe because it wasn't worth the effort—
the machines were on Shyam's side, shrieking
madly, and the TV joined in. Without rain, the
humidity in Médine was sixty-five percent, the
first tractor convoys were leaving Kosovo, and
even if she tried, no sound would come out,
Shyam would choke her and leave her next to the
man on the billiard table; she felt his hand grop-
ing beneath her dress as he pushed her against the
bar. Her head sank into a cluster of silk forget-
me-nots and even through the garnet velvet dress
she could feel Shyam's hot breath on her breasts.
On the shelf above, the bearded Creole statue
watched Shyam's assault with its saintly smile
while the fan whirred. Santee saw a fireball blaze
across the room from the shard of a shattered
windowpane, the plastic chandeliers revealed
unruly reflections, and the ball crashed into one
of the pinball machines with a fiery splatter. The
saint's face reddened. She grabbed the fan's power
cord, yanked, and watched the blades tilt toward
her and scrape the statue, tearing the tinsel off. It

became a jumbled mess and the saint fell toward them, the fan his halo. It was coming for her to punish her as she lay amid the flowers on the bar with Shyam's face in her neck as his hands unbuttoned his pants—once you got on the wrong side of these sorts of saints you were done for. But she had time enough to decide that she hadn't done anything to deserve this fate; that this random saint should have given the matter more thought, and seen that Ram had abandoned her. She saw the bust go sailing past, just an inch or two from her face, flashing his smile in that last second as if to say that saints always do exactly as they please.

Spread-eagle next to the stool, Shyam gaped at her. He groggily brought his hand to his head, then gawked at his fingers covered in plaster dust and a reddish liquid. Santee hurtled toward the door, her high heels clip-clopping. She kept her eyes on Shyam; he pulled himself up unsteadily, screeched something that was half obscenity and half cry of pain. His penis hung out of his pants. She scrambled down the steps with a howl. The heat rising from the street softened her screams, slowed her steps. And maybe it did for Shyam too, although she didn't want to look back to see. It took her some time to reach the main street. A cab drifting past pulled up next to her, its brights on. A yellow cab rather like a tank—a model Santee didn't recognize. The door opened, she heard or thought she heard a gruff voice saying get in, and she threw herself head-long onto the seat. She felt the car speeding up, pressing her deeper into the seat as she lay there, her ear flat against the cool imitation leather. She pulled her knees up and curled into a fetal position; the garnet dress split along its full length with a ripping sound that she thought was her whole body tearing apart. The driver's head was shaved, and all she could see was a white bulge scored by folds of skin on his nape. He was a big man with a drawling, somewhat hoarse voice. She noticed his fingers on the steering wheel were holding an odd-looking cigarette, and he spat the smoke out the window in the middle of his sentences. She didn't absorb what he was saying as she lay there, burrowed into the seat, all she took in was the smell of the sickly-sweet smoke, the smell of Ram's world that seeped into every crevice of the car. She didn't want to sit up, she'd end up Shyam's prey again, he'd track her, see her through the rear window; she didn't want to see the trickle of blood mixed with the Creole saint's plaster, she didn't want to see Shyam's erection. What she wanted was to stay put, her nostrils taking in the white driver's smoke without inhaling, her ear pressed down above the huge cab's well-oiled transmission. But she shouldn't lie there like a baby, she should sit up straight, properly, the way one should in a car driven by a white man. This simply wasn't done, she had to sit up like Ma when she went to visit Uncle Vijay, she shouldn't curl up like this in front of a stranger, or even in front of people she knew—Ma always insisted on her being ladylike.

She had to be able to see Ram walking in the dark if they happened to drive past him.

Don't lie down like that, Shakuntala, the white man's deep, hoarse voice rumbled, you won't be able to enjoy the scenery, and you're not going to get a second chance, tonight is a special night. Santee pushed herself up with her elbows, straightened her back, smoothed out her dress. She dared to look back. Shyam hadn't followed the car, he was standing in the street and watching the Négus burn. The sidewalk teemed with onlookers drawn like moths to the light. She wanted the cab driver to slow down so they could watch the inferno for a bit as well. Maybe Shyam would actually listen now; maybe she could explain that the fire wasn't her or Ram's doing, tell him she'd heard yells on the street, and it had to be the man's friends who had thrown the Molotov cocktails, who were still doing so, even though the Négus was now wholly ablaze and Shyam could see it all. The cab was bearing her farther and farther away from the Négus; she wouldn't get to see that sweet Chinese woman again, or when she did, it would be in front of the Négus with all its flowers reduced to an ash heap roped off by the police. Now, if nothing else, she wanted to at least see the face of the cab driver with his shiny shaved head, but it was nowhere near the review mirror; he was driving with his forehead almost pressed to the window as if to inhale the night air. Maybe he had no face and if he happened to turn his head, what she would see would be as smooth as a globe. The man turned on the radio, unleashing Bob Marley's reedy voice, *I got to have kaya now, got to have kaya now...* Multicolored lights on the dashboard mirrored the singer's weary tones. On the rear window, other lights flared with the slightest tap on the brakes, strobing with green glimmers. You'll never have another night like this one, Shakuntala, it's one of those nights that pulls you outside. I'm not the one telling you not to lie down—the night's what needs you. It needs people to keep it company; after all, they're starting fires here and there and everywhere. Santee had never experienced the city at night. In fact, she had never experienced night at all. Night always locked them in the Bienvenue house, where she'd hear Ram moving around in the other room. He never went to bed right away. What he actually did after sundown was a mystery, she'd fall asleep first and never wake up until the night was gone. Ma always came back from weddings early, blaming her age and her health. One time, she'd taken Santee and Ram along to a funeral vigil in Vallée des Prêtres, and they'd stayed until ten listening to the mourners. The highway back home went right past Port-Louis, nearing but not touching it. Santee still remembered the din of factories despite seeing barely any people—who worked so late at night?—and floodlit, empty parking lots. At the end of the Place d'Armes was the old, sinister government building, and facing it had been a Chinese trawler moored all by itself in the port. She had shaken Ram, asleep with his head on her knees, so he could see. Their uncle had slowed down and she'd been able to read the boat's name:

Ming Sing. Ram had gotten up, looked around as if he knew where they were, groaned, and with deep breaths, laid back down, his small hot cheek pressed against Santee's leg.

You're my first tonight, Shakuntala. The others already left to meet their johns all the way up in Grand-Baie. But they always try to make short work of it so they can come back and sleep, they stare at me if I suggest a little outing, they insist on being paid. He let out a guffaw and a few more puffs of smoke. Santee would never have dreamed of asking a white driver for money.

I knew the day would come when someone good would come down the stairs of the Négus. I waited every night, I practiced what I'd say in my head—sometimes I was so pleased with my spiel, I'd stay parked by the steps for just a bit longer. I'd say: Get in quick, my love, I've been waiting for you. Or maybe I'd just say: Buongiorno Principessa! and those would be the magic words for everything else to happen. I'd rev the motor and we'd be off. I'd show her around town, I'd run all the stoplights so she'd know there was nothing she couldn't ask for, but in the end the only thing she'd ask me, just to be polite, would be: How much do I owe you for the fare? and we'd have

ourselves a good laugh. She wouldn't even ask,
actually, because she'd know, she'd just whisper:
What if we stopped here? And I don't know what
exactly we'd do next, I haven't thought that far…
But we're off and away, aren't we, Shakuntala? Yes,
we're in the dream already… I didn't expect *you* at
all, no, not at all, I hadn't been expecting a Malbar
tonight, not when the girls I drive to Grand-Baie
and back are all Madras. I've only seen one of you
in an Indian film, and that was by accident, I was at
the Scala up in Plaines des Papayes to see a porno,
but I got the times wrong. So I had to settle for
one of your duds where the men all roll around
like gorillas in heat. But the women… I watched
that movie over and over, I don't know how many
times, until they began showing *Titanic* instead.
Shakuntala. And he started laughing and cough-
ing. It was a smoker's raspy laugh, a conspirato-
rial laugh meant to remind her that they were off
and away, that they were going to go around the
world, or at least around what they could conceive
of the world. The laugh she tried to let out in return fell flat; all she could muster in the wake of
the Négus was a wan smile.

   This is actually happening, I can't believe it,
you're in my backseat and I'm driving you, I can't

believe it. He shook his head, but not enough for her to see his face.

Shall we go to the theater, Shakuntala? He swerved left sharply. Santee hadn't recognized the Rose-Hill town center, where she'd been several times with Ma, she hadn't seen the dark mass of Notre-Dame-de-Lourdes or Montmartre's spire sliding past, and now the cab was turning off toward the Plaza. The huge, drab wooden building was all lit up, with its rows of palm trees. A group of people sat on the steps, chatting. The cab slowed, slyly pulled up to the front steps. See, they're out, too, I told you we'll never see another night like this one. People are just like big game… have you ever gone deer hunting, Shakuntala? If there's time I'll take you to Rivière-Noire, there's a place to hunt there, it's off limits at night but I know somebody, I can get you in. You'll see the eyes, so many eyes, eyes always there, none of them ever move when the headlights are shining in their faces, but then they dash off and jump over obstacles in the dark—all you see are small eyes that leap and then disappear into the woods. Characters in a play are no different. See, there isn't much of an audience tonight, so for once they're venturing out.

The onlookers seemed wary. Every now and then, one of the characters would stand up and intone a few lines, half song and half speech, while the others barely reacted. The cab didn't make much noise—it was an old '50s model, as bulky yet quiet as an idling speedboat. When the wind carried the motor's rumble their way, they all looked worriedly at them. Santee didn't know what play they were performing, couldn't read the title on the massive marquee. The actors, some in uniforms, others in long gowns or rags, rushed to the cab. They showed no fear, so Santee figured they must know the driver. A woman and a little girl in tatters piped up: Robert de Noir! But what are you doing out and about? You ought to be home. I could ask you the same, Cosette. And the woman retorted, the little girl echoing her: I'm just waiting for the audience. The reply came with a chuckle: Well, I'm off to find it. You coming with us, Cosette? No, I can't, he told me I didn't belong up on the barricades, they both said, turning to a heavyset old man in a frock coat. Well, keep him company then, Robert de Noir said. He gestured toward the backseat and added, I'm not free tonight. Santee peered at the man with the frock coat; he hadn't come over and instead was eating popcorn on the steps. The actors surrounding the car blocked her view. They peered at her, sitting in the back of Robert de Noir's cab, trying to look prim in her torn dress. This is no night for theater, Robert de Noir declared as he rolled up the window, all the drama's outside. He revved the car and tapped his foot gently on the gas to make his way through the group. The cab was now moving past the Plaza and the Coignet's looming Chinese banyans. Ahead of them were police sirens and a traffic jam. Piles of tires were burning along the roadside but nobody seemed to care. And farther up, a three-story house was on fire. Robert de Noir parked the car and turned up the radio as he asked, without looking at her: You weren't planning on missing this sight, were you?

The fire had almost completely wiped out the top floor, and only the bare window frames remained. Firemen in yellow uniforms were aiming jets of water at the lower floors, but the blaze was so ferocious that to Santee it looked like they were actually spraying fuel on the flames.

They had a front-row spot for the spectacle. Robert de Noir reclined his seat and reached over his shoulder to hand her a packet of peanuts. Enjoy, Shakuntala, even in your Bollywood films there's no way they'd be able to pull off something like that—they'd burn a cardboard cutout or light some fireworks, sure, but *that*... The windows shattered in the heat and shards sprinkled the firefighters' helmets like confetti. In Robert de Noir's cab, parked on the sidewalk, Santee savored the salt of the peanuts on her lips. She took in the crowd, just inches away, eager to see Kent's on fire. The car's glass insulated her from the men— their heat, their touch, but not their gaze. Robert seemed oblivious to them; he had kicked back in his seat, his feet up on the dashboard: bare feet with long, pale toes. She heard him chewing and watched his jaw moving calmly. He was proud of her, proud to have her in the backseat, eating peanuts with him. She started cracking the shells and crunching them loudly so he would know she appreciated the peanuts at least, adding to the pile of empty hulls on the seat. Are you thirsty? I'd have taken you to Kent's, but... He let out a hearty guffaw and had to catch his breath before saying: But it's on fire! That's Kent's. You didn't even recognize it, dear Shakuntala, that used to be Kent's... And then she noticed the ruined Coke bottle sign on the side of the building. The flames had already started on its neck and the water the firefighters were spraying filled what remained of the bottle's body. Her thirst made the decision for Robert de Noir. He yanked the back of his seat up hastily and started the engine. The cab jolted forward, narrowly missing a conflagration on the street, and then did a U-turn as other cars honked. Were they really objecting? There was no stopping a cab in Rose-Hill. Maybe the honking was to make the taxi bounce on its thickly padded suspension. She wanted to tell him it would be nice to stay a bit longer, tucked in the backseat as the folks gawked at the blaze. And surely Ram had to be here, this was the sort of scene he loved; when they set the sugar fields on fire he had been so excited and had run from the house to see. Ma had gone over too, but to shout at the Bienvenue workers to start the backfire fast. Santee could convince Ram to get in the cab, could ask Robert to drop them off in Bienvenue. It would upset Robert, she knew, but her job was to find her little brother and tell Ma...tell her what? She wasn't sure. It was too late, there was no point in fantasizing, Robert de Noir had already turned onto the street past the shoe repair shop, urged onward by a need to quench her thirst. There won't be anything left in town for us to drink if we don't go now, I'm not driving my beautiful Shakuntala to any old joint. Robert ran the red lights as if every second counted, as if he were driving someone badly injured. He sped down Vandermeersch Street, the speakers blaring at each corner, *got to have kaya now*, he yelled at anyone standing in the way of his mission to slake his passenger's thirst. In the Beau-Bassin town center all they found was a restaurant being looted, people climbing out with armfuls of bottles and leaving nothing behind. Robert de Noir's irritation only grew and he kept on swearing. He dismissed Gool's tea room. Why didn't he ask her? Why? She'd have been perfectly happy with a warm-white vanilla tea with lots of sugar. Robert went the wrong way around the roundabout in front of the church toward the part of town with all the nice houses, but they wouldn't find Ram there. She didn't mention this to him, but yawned instead, and this was such an affront that he couldn't bring himself to point out his family home, with its glassed-in verandah and flowerbeds full of petunias. He wondered how he could even have shown her without her making fun of him, of that bourgeois cottage, but he didn't linger on the thought. He drove past the new, white mosque, holding his tongue rather than voicing the fury that the riotous, incessant calls to prayer stirred up in him. Better for Robert de Noir to keep silent. He had realized that showing a starlet around was a difficult job and life was unfair. Next to the metal railing in front of the monastery, by the sign indicating private property, he slowed for a second, just one second, which was the evening's undoing—showing a Shakuntala around meant never pausing, meant all doors were open for you. The drive snaked between flowerbeds of bamboo orchids and when they reached the wooden bridge he stopped. The headlights shone on the Tour Blanche, which had been inhabited by the monks of the order of Saint Expédit ever since the death of the lady of the castle. Robert's concern was evident as he stepped out, leaving the engine running. Huge trunks Santee had taken for palm trees slowly started moving in the darkness, and a large animal disappeared behind the outbuildings. She looked at Robert for an explanation. He was crouching by the stream's bank. It was the same posture as that of the washerwomen in Bienvenue: legs spread apart, skirts gathered between. His bald scalp gleamed in the moonlight, but she couldn't see what he was doing, he had his back to her. There was a deer's head embroidered on his gray suede shirt, and he was wearing velvet pants of the same color. She had never seen anyone dressed like that. On the sugar estate near Bienvenue the whites wore khakis when they weren't in the fields, though they weren't taxi drivers. His name was engraved on a small bronze plaque affixed to the dashboard's varnished walnut: *Robert de Noir, vicomte de Beau-Bassin.* A coat of arms with the same design as on his shirt, and a medallion of Saint Christopher carrying the baby Jesus on his shoulder caught Santee's attention as she clambered over the seat to sit up front. She slipped into the too-deep driver's seat and tried to touch the pedals with her toes, but to no avail. Then she squatted down and pressed the accelerator with her hand. The engine roared with pleasure.

Robert de Noir jumped as he heard his car revving. He ran over with water held in his joined palms and found the small dark red heap in the driver's seat. He felt relief at the fact that she was still there. Waited. As she raised her head, all she saw were his two hands cupped together, the torso disappearing above the roof of the car. She rolled down the window and he brought his hands toward her. She held his fingers and drank the water. It wasn't fresh, the water had a faint taste of treacle, just like the stream behind her house did when they were cleaning the machinery in the sugar factory. He let her take all the time she wanted and, once the water had been drunk, she wiped her face by pressing it into his damp hands. She felt the roughness of his joints as if it were her face covering his hands and not the other way around. His fingers trembled against her eyelids. Then she leaned back onto the passenger seat and shut her eyes. Lights were coming on in the Gothic windows of the monastery. Robert slipped nimbly into the car. I have to find my brother. The shrillness of her voice struck him; she kept her eyes shut with a determination that said, matter-of-factly, what he had always suspected: you'll drop me off wherever we find him. He was disappointed; he had been hoping for such a long time for a night free of orders.

He would have liked to keep watching her with her head slumped toward the door as she slept more deeply. The car dodged a monk-mahout brandishing a lantern—Stop! Stop!—and headed out. Why couldn't he offer her a show of sounds and lights, sweep the headlights across the small pond, feed the eels, whisper that when his

mother was little she had played badminton on a
mown portion of this vast estate? Why? Because
Shakuntala didn't care about mothers, and she
only pretended to be worried about her brother,
but he wasn't fooled, he'd seen others like her.
Her brother! She could have come up with something better, told him there was someone else
in her life, someone waiting for her. She could
have confessed while he'd had his back to her, she
could have told him what she really wanted: the
fire. He'd been driving her around in his own cab
unthinkingly. Her brother... If she had told him
the truth, she could have gotten out of the cab,
looked him in the eye, and given him the order,
even though only people who are weak give orders
as they look up for inspiration. Shakuntala ought
to have confided something, anything, to him; he,
Robert de Noir, hadn't held anything back.

The wind blowing through the wide-open driver's door was no match for the harsh sun. Dark
blotches of sweat discolored the garnet velvet
dress. The Cresta was all alone at the end of the
Place de la Gare, parked in the bus lane. No more
music flowed from the radio; it was now repeating

the latest about the high-pressure weather system. Inside the car it was stifling, but Santee didn't dare get out and make her way across the square. In the distance, past the asphalt and concrete, a man who wasn't Robert de Noir was strutting from building to building.

She knew the square from having been there many times with Ma, shopping before the holidays, but today all the metal grates were lowered. Ma always headed straight to the shops, while Santee wanted to take her time, pick out all the sounds, get a sense of the place, but that was how things were with Ma, the older you get the less time there is to waste, and the sounds aren't going anywhere after all. Santee didn't remember a thing about getting off the bus to pick up Ram. She didn't even know whether that had been just yesterday, if she'd taken the time then, alone at last, to absorb the sounds of the Place de la Gare. She must have, that would be why she'd missed her little brother. What she did remember was the young conductor warning her, it had stuck in her head as she'd gotten off the bus. And also a weird rumor that the last buses headed east had been leaving the station, that there already weren't any more headed north, the roads that way had already been blockaded. People had been talking about strangers and lootings, you needed to be careful going in that direction, assuming you'd even want to. Santee knew that she was now in Ram's world, and that finding him here would be no easy feat. In the overheated cab, she tried to recall when she had seen her brother last.

The young man at the other end of the square was sitting on the sidewalk. He was looking at the cab with all its chrome gleaming in the sun; he had to have seen her moving. Sleeping. Maybe even heard her breathing. Because nothing else in the square was moving. All she could make out was his hunched-over, wary profile, as if he were actually scared of being noticed by the car's occupant. Or by someone else. The rising hum of traffic brought some semblance of normalcy, although it was late in the morning for people to be heading out. So many things seemed to be out of sorts, like sugarcane stunted by a too-dry summer, or little brothers gone astray. The sun might have risen, but day hadn't really broken. A metallic scraping echoed amid the empty storefronts. The teenager started. Behind him, a few men were working at the steel grate of a clothing store. He got up, looking torn. Scratched his head, took a few steps toward the group, which gave him a hearty hello. Then, changing his mind, he headed for the car with his hands in the pockets of his shorts, moving at an exaggeratedly calm pace. He turned around every so often to see where the others were. They shouted at him. The metal slats had slipped from their tracks. Santee realized she didn't have much time and got out of the car. The guy was now running. His calves bulged; she could see his grimace in the shadow cast by his hat's brim. He didn't stop when he reached her, he grabbed her by the arm and began dragging her. The group had come back out onto the square and noticed the car. They were all about the same age as the guy in shorts, nineteen or twenty, and they ambled along unhurriedly. The man pulled Santee across the green along Vandermeersch Street and then slipped into the passageway under the old railroad tracks. The others had their sights on the abandoned car. They'd popped open all the doors and were making it bounce on its suspension. Once they lost interest, they flipped it over, opened the gas tank, and set it on fire. Santee could hear them shouting, laughing, and chanting long before the flames rose above the sheet-metal roofs. The two made their way down to the road leading past the monastery. He let go of her arm; his fingers had left red marks. Gasping for breath, he asked her where she had been heading, before realizing how ridiculous the question was—where can anyone go in a cab without a driver, where can anyone go when it's been set on fire, where can anyone go when they've been kidnapped? Do you know Ram? was the only response he got. He shrugged. There's dozens of Rams. Let me think, there's Ramon the sheet-metal guy on Hugnin Road, there's Rambo, but nobody's seen him since all the fighting last night, and there's Ramses... She wasn't listening. She'd stopped to pull off her shoes, which were starting to hurt. She sat on a milestone and examined the purplish blister she'd developed from running. I was saying the third one is Ramses, some people call him Ram but some others call him Ses, I only met him once, at a party where we were all drunk, he deejays at the Sphinx. He stopped talking to take a look at the girl. As he stood over her, what he saw was the too-short garnet dress torn along the sides and the thick dark hair spilling over her face as she focused on her blister. Her shoe had fallen into the gutter. He saw girls like this every so often—they'd come from the villages to find work, but at night. Pimps were always busy driving Creole girls back to the countryside in the wee hours. But this girl was Indian; she'd been left behind in the night. He'd never been with an Indian girl; he didn't go looking for them like some of the guys from Trèfles who fantasized about unwrapping their saris. He thought of Indian girls as timid, awkward, unsophisticated. He wouldn't want his friends to see him with this girl who had purple blisters, limping in what was left of her dress. The women in his part of town hadn't gone outside in two days; their mothers had kept them at home. They were listening to CDs of Kaya, the singer who'd been found dead in his jail cell. They kept repeating his lines that called for more justice, for sime la limiere, while the guys went out and protested his death by throwing rocks at the police stations and setting grocery stores on fire. It was a blister on the side of her little toe that she was trying to rub away. He wondered if she would be able to walk around Rose-Hill with that—nobody just walked around Rose-Hill any old way, everyone here knew that, and those who came from the villages learned it fast. Everyone wore the right shoes, the right clothes, they got it all at the Galerie or at the Arcades, or in a pinch, from one of the stalls in Arab Town. The idea to get her all that came out of nowhere, he'd never asked a girl if he could buy her clothes before. He didn't know anything about women's clothes, and he'd never have dared to suggest she change her dress. He had no idea how a woman would take such an offer. One time he'd said something to a girl about her nail polish, just a passing comment for no real reason, and she'd ended up sobbing. In the middle of the street in Rose-Hill. And everybody had stared at him, and the girl had just kept crying for effect. The memory was painful enough that the only thing he felt comfortable doing was sitting next to her, right in the gutter, next to her long, bare legs, and waiting patiently until she finished with her blister. She crinkled her forehead and every so often, when she wanted to rest her eyes, she batted her long lashes while her mascara ran in streaks down her cheeks. He couldn't tell if the worst of the pain was gone now. She finally noticed his presence and looked at him. He let her, allowed her to take in his small cross earring, the stubble of a two-day beard barely thicker than his buzzed hair. As her gaze reached his face, his eyes, he looked away. On his forearm was a tattoo that read RONALDO MILAN AC. She suddenly felt embarrassed for stopping to deal with her pain and making him wait. But the guy didn't seem terribly upset at her, they were comfortable in the shadow of some bamboo, their feet in the gutter. The house visible through the tall stalks was quiet, those within it hadn't bothered to wake up yet, maybe they would wake early tomorrow, or maybe they wouldn't ever again—even though this was a morning not to be missed. Santee felt like she should have a tattoo with her name, too, it would save her all those introductions she could never stand. She'd go quiet while Ma introduced her as mo tifi, never Santee, and afterward, nobody ever said her name, she was just Ma's daughter. It surely wouldn't be long now before Ram insisted on getting a tattoo of his name on his forearm just like this Ronaldo Milanac.

Ro-nal-do Mi-la-nac...

What did you say? Your name, it's a nice name. He didn't pay her any attention; he picked up the shoe to see what it was made of. No surprise that she was having trouble with it—it was a brand-new black pleather thing as stiff as cardboard. Do you want new ones? That had to mean she'd get two new pairs in as many days. Why was he going to all this trouble for her? Santee, in turn, had quickly learned not to deal with questions, there was no use in asking them in Ram's world, where you had to just go for it, and that was what Ram did, with animal instinct. Well, it looks like you need new ones, Ronaldo Milanac said, and then he tried to grab her by the arm like he had before. There isn't any time to lose. But she pushed him off. She glumly put her shoe back on as best as she could, made a face, got up, and started walking again determinedly; after a few steps, she was leaning against him again. Coming out onto Royal Road with her hanging from his arm, he looked all around, embarrassed. A group of women were coming back from Beau-Bassin, pushing grocery store carts that jangled and clattered, heaped with provisions. Nobody noticed the two of them, and he couldn't leave this faltering girl to her own devices with the town turned upside down. The night before, he'd been out with his friends and everything had been perfect, they'd raided a gas station, flipped over no less than six cars and, to top it off, out by Chebel they'd tackled a bus and the police hadn't been able to drag away its carcass until nearly midnight. He was helpless now as he watched her pry off her shoes and walk barefoot on the cobblestones. The coolness seemed to soothe her and she slowed her pace: there was no rush anymore. You don't have to, it's okay, she said. He looked around. The women were walking right past them, talking loudly, the oldest one scolding the others for having rushed, for not having taken the time to pick and choose. The others laughed to themselves and pushed their carts this way and that. They were laden with frozen food, chickens, and cuts of meat that dripped a trail along the ground. If they followed this blood-tinged trail back, would they reach some source of plenty? Ronaldo hardly seemed to need this lead. She let him take her hand this time and, together, they crossed Royal Road. He led her straight to the Arcades. Other people were coming out, their carts jangling and clattering as well, but rather than wade right into the crowd in front of the grocery store, he turned off toward the clothing shops. Here, everything was still calm, and a subdued light bathed the boutique's slender mannequins and its sprays of dried flowers. Santee rushed over to look. Multicolored T-shirts hung from a dead tree and pink and yellow and green shoes and sunglasses lay, as if washed in with the tide, on a stretch of sawdust standing in for a beach. In the background was the frozen burble of a sapphire sea. Ronaldo Milanac had vanished, thank goodness, now she could take all the time she wanted. The darkened passageway seemed to be empty; maybe Ronaldo was gone for good and now there was just her, the shriveled tree, and its blazingly colorful fruit. These clothes couldn't be for sale. The clothes her mother bought were always stacked in display cases with the price tag on top, in piles to make more room; the salespeople went up and down the aisles with a wary look; you were supposed to haggle like Ma, she did it so well that she always came home from her errands in Rose-Hill with a delighted glint in her eyes behind her old tortoiseshell glasses. The sellers, either out of pity because they took country people for idiots or, more likely, just to get this pain in the neck out of there, played along and she always came back to Bienvenue in no time with all her steals in her arms. There was no shortage of canny negotiators in the family, all of them firm but fair—Ma's older brother, Uncle Vijay, predicted a brilliant future for Ram as an economist once he was done with school, but Ram wasn't interested

in trade, or money, and Santee found herself wondering what was going on in his head.

A rattling noise marked Milanac's return. He
had a cart of his own now, brimming with jars of
preserves and bottles dripping with condensation.
He hadn't been able to resist the siren song of
the grocery store. You're still here? he asked with
a chuckle. She wasn't charmed. Where did you
think I'd go? He ought to have kept on dream-
ing about stuffing his face and left her alone with
her display. Suddenly remembering that she had
a problem with her shoes, he started rummaging
in the cart. He hefted a jar of preserves but caught
himself and gave it to Santee instead. Go for it—
what's your name? Shakuntala. Well, Shakuntala,
be my guest. Go on! Throw it! You just going to
stand there all day staring at me like that? You
want those shoes or whatever? The first throw at
the thick glass was awkward—the jar bounced
back, barely missing her, and Milanac laughed
heartily. Try again, you've got to earn those shoes,
they look Italian to me, I'm not gonna do it for
you, you think I'm at the beck and call of any lady
I come across? He settled onto the sidewalk in
front of the hair salon next door and pried the
cap off a beer bottle with his teeth. Go for it,

Shakuntala, have at it! Fury rose up in her and she grabbed the jar and threw it with all the anger she had at Milanac, at the blister on her foot, at Ram who threw stones at dogs while she had to clap whenever he hit his target amid the din of animals barking in pain and fear—she threw the jar against the glass. Huge shards rained down and shattered in front of her, and the sawdust beach spilled silently out onto the ground. The smell of the shop, a mix of flowery, fruity scents from a plug-in vaporizer, filled the air and she wanted to absorb it all into her skin, so she took a step forward. He jumped up: Careful! The glass is sharp and the hospital's full! You'd bleed to death, Shakuntala! He yanked her away brusquely, pulled out another jar, and finished the job on the rest of the window. All right, Shakuntala, what are you waiting for? Someone to carry you in? She didn't answer; the blanket of glass in front of the display fascinated her. Well, why not, you don't weigh that much… Leaning over, Ronaldo Milanac picked her up in his arms, his thick sneakers crunching on the shards of glass, and, with one long step, he entered the shop.

The carpeting and fine clothing gave the space a cozy feel. She stood in the middle of the beach, not yet daring to look through the shelves. He headed toward the back to put on some music while she tentatively began to run her fingers over some of the fabrics. Don't forget your kicks, he yelled to her, that's why we're here after all, you can't just walk around barefoot all day. She nodded, grabbing a pair with yellow straps. Ronaldo, now sitting in a beach chair, watched her. He pulled off his shirt to take in a bit of the spotlights' false sun. She came over next to him to try on her shoes; he got down to help her pull the straps tight. A sea breeze, teasing and salty, raised goosebumps on his skin. If you don't like these, just say it now, don't wait until we're out walking again, I'm not planning on coming back. Not planning, not planning—as if it wasn't clear that there was no going back in Ram's town, if there had been, Ram himself would already have come home, shamefaced. She wasn't mad at him anymore, she knew that what she needed to do was keep going until she found him. Back in the rear of the store, Ronaldo Milanac finished off his beer. She insisted that the shoes fit perfectly, but he kept asking, more to get her to walk around in front of him than because he didn't believe her; she took a few more steps, not to prove anything

but just to please him, and then she went back to
the clothes. Take what you want and then we're
going, he said, annoyed that she would abandon
him so quickly, I have better things to do than
wait while you try on clothes, let's wrap it up, take
it all, I'll get you another cart, just get a move
on. She wanted to consider the options, to pluck
the fruits from the dead tree one by one and hold
them up in front of her to see how they looked
in the mirror; she wanted him to tell her what
he liked, to tease her, but the smell of the ocean
was fading, the seaside breeze becoming stifling,
just like the river back in Bienvenue, which sometimes teemed with runoff from the factory—the
water took in everything, there was no use resist-
ing. This was no time to be indecisive, nobody
could stay in the same place for long in Ram's
world, especially not just standing and looking in
a mirror. The black smoke of burning rubber filled
the Arcades; Ronaldo got up hurriedly, pricking
up his ears, We'd better shove off now, come on,
quick, let's go, they grabbed random armfuls of
clothes, T-shirts and swimsuits, saris, straw hats.
We forgot the necklaces, just one necklace. Okay,
okay, but come on, let's go, they knocked over the
dead tree as they went out through the display

window. She wasn't upset about leaving the store, didn't glance at the madras prints on the ground, the scattered hangers, the eroded beach. Once the clothes were knotted in a bundle, they threw them in the cart and went out onto the street. Shouts from amid the smoke of the grocery store, a siren. People had started running again, they all felt that impulse every so often to hurry. The two started moving more quickly too, working together to push the cart. There was still laughter amid the shouts, but it was becoming more strained. He decided to go down one of the sloping alleys, and they had to lean back with their whole bodies to slow the cart down. Other people with carts were headed the same way, the siren was getting closer, shriller; she occasionally turned around to see but there was nothing there, Don't look back, there's no use, you'll make the cart tip over, we just have to keep going even if we can't see. The others were trading jokes as they raced—matri-archs, a guy in a business suit with an armful of dishwasher detergent—and she could hear bits and pieces amid their panting. People were telling jokes and others were piping up with the punch-line, and as they ran they introduced themselves: Oh yes, you're the one I saw at Moody's, you're

Jennifer's cousin… The road forked, some went in the direction of Beau-Bassin to try to get to Cité Barkly, others headed for the swanky part of the Cascade. The siren caught up to them. It turned out to be an ambulance with a mangled body in the back, a gray pair of pants with odd creases, bare feet that were totally white. The poor thing, who knows what happened to him, He jumped from the spire of the Église Montmartre. His head was shaved, his face no longer visible under the oxygen mask that a nurse had fastened absentmindedly, her attention more on a colleague holding a bag of saline solution. Santee made Ronaldo stop to watch the big white body go past, the guy in the cab had been big, but he couldn't have been this big, maybe bodies steeped in Ram's town all grew to match the size of the vehicles they were in. They got going again, pushing the cart together; she felt weaker; they had to pay attention so they didn't follow the others down the side roads, down slopes that were gentler and more alluring. They went toward Le Pouce mountain, why that way and not any other he didn't say. He couldn't possibly know that, the night before, she had come down this exact same path; no, it couldn't have been the same one, in the cab driven

by what was his name again—these were empty
days, days without memory, and, every morning,
everything started all over again on a different
track. She couldn't possibly know for sure either.
Through the sweat trickling into her eyes she
saw only the vague shapes of trees, houses, and
some stretch of pavement ahead. She was holding the cart back with both hands, letting herself
be pulled forward, and at the same time she was
yoking herself to Ronaldo Milanac in their effort.
She could smell apples and alcohol, but also other
smells, less remarkable ones amid the groceries.
She heard his anxious panting in her ear as he
told her they had to put as much distance as possible between them and the others—that was the
best thing to do, these were new days, days full of
promise.

We can't go any farther, she protested, only
to hear, No, we can. She could feel the cart draw-
ing them forward, downward, toward the coast;
they'd never have the strength to push the cart up
back toward Rose-Hill. But why do we have to
go back there, anyway? Ronaldo Milanac had no
good answer, they had to go back, pure and sim-
ple, but for the moment they stopped. Ronaldo's
weariness surprised her—she could have kept on

pushing the cart with him forever. He was pale and struggling to keep his hold on the cart so that it wouldn't go sailing off without them if she let go. It was tempting to let this overloaded cart pull him, it would be so much easier to stop making decisions and just go with the flow. She left Ronaldo Milanac to dwell in his thoughts and peered between the slats of the fence to their right. The shoddily squared-off planks were worm-eaten and stood atop a rather low wall of rough stones. Little could be seen from the road; people would have to do what she was doing— wedge their eyes between the loose boards. He heard her whispering: I can see trees and ponds and fish in them, I can see children yelling, but he couldn't hear anything else apart from his own pulse pounding dully. That's the Balfour Garden, he said. She repeated, I can see trees and lawns, so many palm trees, Yes, I know, if you want to, we can go in there, I'm sure they have birds and deer in enclosures, your choice, we can go... It didn't seem like a bad idea at all. She wanted to make him smile, We'll be able to relax there for a few minutes.

He knew the Balfour Garden well, nothing particularly unexpected would happen there, it

would be nice to introduce this girl from the villages to the garden. He looked around, they were
alone and nobody had followed them. The gate
was open. They struggled to get the cart up the
steps onto the stone path. Between the rows of
thief palms and clumps of bougainvillea were
sandpits and playhouses, but not a single child.
She walked up to a swing that was still brightly
colored despite its flaking paint; he waited for her
to climb on, or to lean on him to get to the top
of the slide, but she was the one to hold back this
time, she wouldn't do it. She ran her fingers over
the rougher spots on the ropes and gave the seat
a few small pushes. Then she made up her mind
and kept on going down the path. She's got to be
thinking about her missing brother, he thought,
unaware that Ram had always refused to get on
a swing, to the great annoyance of Pa who had
bought him a brand-new one. Come on already,
she said, running ahead of him as he wearily
pushed the cart over the stone slabs, and before
long she had disappeared around the bend past
a row of bottle palms. When he had her in his
sights again, she had stopped at the railing by the
cliff. Her belly was pressed against the wooden
crossbeams and her chest was thrust out over the

abyss like an animal's. There was no question in his mind that if not for the barrier she would have instinctively gone flying into the grayish green stretches of the Grande Rivière's gorges. A few expansive seconds hovering above the sugarcane fields and looking out over the far slope, like the trickling waterfall, an unmoving, almost transparent line not unlike the Tour Blanche, set right in the middle of its lawn more than a century ago; then, suddenly, everything would start moving again, not just her plunging into the abyss, but also the creepers and the wind, the tropicbirds with their shrill cries. The far-off river that had been dry for months would start flowing again. She leaned over the railing, her arms windmilling like a drowning swimmer's, and he was certain she was going to throw herself over. He left the cart and rushed over, grabbed her by the waist, and pulled her away as she fought against him. Her eyes were blazing, but he held firm. It took some time for her to calm down, for the tropicbirds to turn their gazes skyward again, for the monks to go back to walking peacefully under the banyans. Her eyes lingered on the Tour Blanche for a while longer, then she calmly pulled away from Ronaldo Milanac, her last anchor. She tottered to the treacly stream, Watch out, it's slippery, the mud's disgusting, be careful with your new shoes, but his words came too late, the sludge was already up to her ankles. He found himself a spot in the shade of a flame tree. The beer was still cold and he nestled between the buttressing roots, his legs splayed out. No use trying to make sense of girls, he'd brought plenty of them here, sometimes they'd cry, sometimes they'd tell him all sorts of ridiculous hopes and dreams. They were like all the plants in this garden, each one blooming in its own season. This one was drinking water from the stream, which flowed from the Trianon factory, and just thinking about it was enough to put him off his beer. He could only see her butt, as small as a child's ball, hidden among the taro vine leaves, but then she stood up again. She cupped some water in her hands, splashed it on her face, her hair, her arms. Maybe it was a rite, he thought, something Malbars did in accordance with their religion, like walking on hot coals or pricking their cheeks with needles. That was an explanation that fit her in her place, like the river in its bed, or a tortoise in its shell. This life was pleasant enough, but it beat a silent, throbbing rhythm in his body like a voice reaching the limits of falsetto. He started to regret not having gone back to the others in the town center.

She found him asleep in a despair of sorts among the tree's sheltering roots. The bottle of beer had rolled out of his open hand, emptying in a foam on the grass. She stayed there, standing and watching him at rest, in contrast to the morning's feverishness—approachable and vulnerable. His mouth was half open, revealing his teeth, and a smirk she had originally taken for a smile stretched his face. It reminded her of Ram's slight grimace of pain or surprise when she extracted splinters from his finger with a needle. Ram never voiced his discomfort, she wondered how he did that, she always let out a scream at the least pain. She wondered what hurt for boys, what made them squeeze their eyes shut. She could make out the sturdy torso in the vee of his undershirt, just enough to see one nipple and his ribs exhaling peacefully. She watched this steady breathing a while longer, then went to see what the cart held. She didn't dare to pull it closer and make it jangle.

He woke up to a spread of cookies, apple juice boxes, beer bottles, and smoked sausage. For lack of a picnic blanket, she had laid out several T-shirts. The girl was nowhere to be seen. The impractical shoes with straps had been cast aside. He was so shocked he didn't think to get up, and his eyes went from the empty cart that gleamed in the sun to the food surrounding him. His surprise gave way to anger once he realized that the beer bottles were getting hot. He leaped up to go to the river and stick them in the water. She was definitely gone, and had left him there in the middle of a picnic he hadn't asked for. This wasn't even the first time—once a girl named Caroline had abandoned him here, almost naked, hurling insults at him after having led him on all morning. This time, he'd run and catch her and tell her what he really thought, about women, what he had to say about all the time he wasted on them, what did it matter if grocery stores were being set on fire in town right then? He was furious at himself for having fallen asleep in front of her.

Another woman appeared, clearly to protect the first one or to finish off her job, pushing apart the branches of a eucalyptus like a timid doe. But he was the one who felt unsafe in this garden. She wore a long linen dress and had flowers in her hair. She was cautious as she walked barefoot, looking for the surest spots. She examined the items under the flame tree, looked around, then, finally seeing him at the stream's edge, seemed to be relieved. She went to sit by the tree and wait for him. He started laughing—a vulgar, astonished laugh. A defeated laugh that touched her. Not having any better option, he went and joined her where the food had been laid out for this meal, under this tree, in this place. She opened a bag of potato chips, licking the salt off her fingers. He had never eaten ham with dried fruit, never drunk whiskey from the bottle. Nor had she. They didn't wait until they'd had their fill to get up. She pulled him down the path and he followed, laughing. Sometimes she would disappear behind the palm-tree trunks, then her sweet face would peek out, Shakuntala, Shakuntala, what do you want? Deep down, it was as if the sitar were emitting its first quavering notes. The only shows he'd ever bothered to watch on TV had been American, and so he had no idea how to follow her among the lotus ponds like those Bombay actors—he'd have caught her too quickly, ruined the whole thing. With the bottle of scotch in his hand, he shuffled awkwardly down the path, not yet convinced that he should just follow. But she never lost hope, her acrobatic twirls grew more and more lascivious, her eyes quivered to suggest that she'd soon need a strong hand to keep her from falling, and the circles she traced around him tightened. Her interlocked fingers and the rhythm of her pace belied so many emotions that were just as new for her. They slipped unknowingly into figures of Bollywood choreography, he felt at ease in the snare of her hair, and fell with her into the garden's green grass. They stayed there a moment, unmoving, then rolled down the lawn to the cliff's edge; she whispered words he'd never heard before, explained with a bat of her eyelashes, a crook of her neck. He told her the story of the Tour Blanche, haunted by the soul of some old scholar, a British one and a mad one too. She interrupted him—of course Shakuntala knew about the Tour Blanche. He wanted to let her keep going, to hear her chatter the way Bengalis did, but all that remained of the Tour Blanche was the funny taste on her tongue of the stream water that she shared with him. Along with the name she had revealed: Shakuntala. He didn't let himself get swept up, telling her how the scholar had claimed that humans had descended from monkeys and had ended up trying to talk to macaques in the ravine. They both laughed, alone in the garden, lying on the grass beneath the bottle

palms. It was a garden for laughter just outside
the town on fire, each one's hand was gentle on
the other's skin, their breaths mingled, those were
days with no yesterday, days with no tomorrow,
and there was no telling who took the other.

The British scholar's notes mentioned an
elephant on the grounds of the Tour Blanche.
Why not lions, gazelles, a snake? Serpents were
a familiar presence in gardens, a reminder that
everything was fleeting. Elephants, on the con-
trary, were meant to last, they were imported from
India to the colonies to pull heavy loads. Ronaldo
Milanac was convinced that the Tour Blanche
one was still alive and the monks were hiding
it from the locals so as not to scare them, but
there were nights when the gardens echoed with
dreadful trumpeting. It was possible, elephants
did have long lives, longer even than turtles, Ram
had insisted—he never stopped asking her tricky
questions taken out of an old encyclopedia. Why
was it that the old scholar had only stayed a short
while at the Tour Blanche? Because he was driven
by his madness to talk to other monkeys or simply because he was exiled from paradise for his
heresy? It had to be both—reason has no place
in gardens. The tame monkeys had come back,

curious, to huddle on the fence and behold the now-sleeping couple. The monkeys watched them, whispering mischievously to each other. They were no longer living their macaque lives in the ravine, jumping from branch to branch for thimbleberries, but had come and invaded this garden where Shakuntala and Ronaldo Milanac had fallen in love with each other, and the creatures let out small sharp cries like badly behaved children. She let go, opened her eyes, and got up, pushing Ronaldo aside. As she stood, furious in her long, rumpled linen dress, she saw Ram among them. They faced off: her with her lover at her feet in the garden grass, him astride the fence. The Tour Blanche presided over their evenly matched duel, and once again the tropicbirds froze in the sky. But the other monkeys dragged Ram away, the power that Princess Shakuntala wielded here among the lotus ponds in the feasting garden was too great. A footpath led away along the other side of the fence, plunged from the garden down to the cliffside aloes. Ronaldo Milanac, lying dazedly on the lawn strewn with bottles, paper bags, spread-out T-shirts, saw the linen dress disappear over the fence. He ran his hand over the flattened grass beside him. The monkey-children's invasion had

cut their Bollywood film short. Maybe, if he'd
been more willing to believe in the old scholar's
story, he might have realized that she was hurtling
down the path to try—as the scholar had—to talk
to the monkeys; as he didn't understand the monkeys' language, the path beyond the fence was un-
known to him. His eyes took in the rubble of the
picnic once more and then he headed for the gate.

Swallowed by a tunnel in which branches
snapping, screams in the distance, and thorns
sliding against one another became whispers
meant for her, she barely felt the acacia bush
pricking her, didn't see the ravine's bottom. Had
that really been Ram on the fence? Each step toward her brother was a step away from Ronaldo
Milanac, from herself, and from returning to
Ma's house in Bienvenue; she was now nothing
but one unexplained disappearance following
another. In the tunnel of thorns and doubts, she
suddenly had a clear picture of the path Ram
had been clearing from the start, taking devilish
pleasure in keeping her at a distance, just like he
did in Bienvenue, in the little garden adjoining
the sugarcane fields behind Ma's house. It always
ended badly, Ma would find her crying in her
room; all Ma had to do was call for him to come

out of whatever nook he'd hidden in, but instead Ma would stare her down as if she'd lost track of him on purpose, as if she were sowing panic throughout the house for no reason. Fury seized her and she rushed onward. The sounds of something trying to get away grew more distinct, she could make out a white shirt amid the fur and a lanky form that had already surrendered. She became aware of her strength in the last few steps that separated the two of them—in the tussle the boy let out a yip, his bare face rent by terror. He was far younger than Ram, but just as delicate. He was sobbing and she felt bad the way she might when catching, nearly hurting a bird or other woodland animal that shouldn't be touched because it would die then and there. She let him go, but it was already too late. The little monkey was dead and it was just some boy's thin legs that flailed as he scrambled up the path to civilization, back to his parents' house, abandoning this wild life because he was just a boy-child in the woods. At a loss for words, she listened to his whimpers receding in the distance. The other noises waned as if the gang had paused to wait for what was next, for the missing monkey to return or for all of them to get caught. But maybe they were gone for good, maybe they'd made their way down the side of the ravine… She got her answer when she started walking, the rustling further down began again, staying well ahead of her. She took care to keep her distance this time; in any case, her descent was slower because all her fury had been replaced by fear. Fear of slipping, as she could feel the path's soft, thick mud between her toes, and fear of scraping her feet on stumps. The sun was past its peak. It could have been early or late, but the darkness was no surprise here at the bottom of the Grande Rivière ravine into which she had followed a gang of child-monkeys. There was no question of going back up, nobody clambered up the cliffs of the Grande Rivière at this late hour, nobody even walked there, and then she fell into the basaltic riverbed with a thud, welcoming the unyielding harshness with relief. Waist-high masses of lava—the only things that broke the surface during floods—rose up here and there on the carpet of pebbles and small, murky puddles. All that remained of the river and its waterfall was a weak whistling amid the clumps of ferns and taro leaves. She scanned the horizon above for the garden fence, but without any luck. The Tour Blanche, too, was hidden behind the cliff's edge. But, down at her level, the child-monkeys were leaping from rock to rock along the river's curve. She didn't dare to do the same, and made her way around the puddles in the pebble bed. Their sharp cries picked up now and then, as if to catch each other's attention and goad each other on. They were unconcerned by her presence, dawdling in their search for some berries or critters like timillions or dark tadpoles that had survived the drought. They weren't scared of her anymore; she had been brought down to their level; they were all at the mercy of Grande Rivière Nord-Ouest, with its massive banks and seasonal surges. She wasn't trying to find Ram anymore, she headed upriver with her mind elsewhere, at Ma's where the tides didn't matter, Ma who never lost track of the days, ritualistically cleaning the house in the morning, meeting the other women at the river after that, feeding the animals at night. Ma was oblivious to low tides, the river's level might fall slightly but it would have no effect on her life. Ma didn't listen to the radio and didn't save water as citizens were asked to. But Santee wasn't only thinking about Ma, she was also thinking about that garden at the top of the cliff with a name she no longer remembered. The song came back to her, stopping her in her tracks:

> *Shakuntala, Shakuntala,*
> *I know nothing but her name,*
> *Shakuntala, Shakuntala,*
> *Not her caste, nor whence she came—*

He had sung it awkwardly in Hindi, unable to recreate its vibratos, just mindlessly repeating the words that everyone—even the Christians—knew from the film. Past the bend, the gorge ended in a rocky outcrop. The Indian song had, unbeknownst to her, brought her closer to the gang of children. They had stopped, assuaged, and looked back. As if home again, they had dispersed among the rocks, checking the nooks for reassurance that the place hadn't changed, that nobody had intruded while they were away. She heard the splashes of diving, laughter and shrieking, splattering and snorting. She hid behind some lava for a while, listening to them. Ram sat alone on a rocky platform, nude, as water from his swim trickled down and pooled around his brown body. Others were playing in the one remaining pool of the Grande Rivière, sprays of foam sputtering every so often onto the outcrop. His legs were pressed to his chest, locked together by his hands. As he rested his chin on his knees, his eyes contemplated the gorges' outlet downstream. He was waiting for something that beckoned from beyond the river's bend. Down that way, she realized, was someplace he'd never been, and the river, or what remained of it, was flowing there, drawn toward some strange fate. Had those muted explosions been meant to herald the river, the way fireworks burst in the sky for newlyweds? It was unlikely they were for this ghost of a stream that last summer's heavy rains had forgotten. The other boys were spread out, some throwing stones to flush something out of a thicket, four others sitting around a flat stone playing dominoes. She heard coins clinking against the stone. She and Ram sometimes played dominoes, but after a few minutes he'd always start yawning. Maybe if there had been money on the line he wouldn't have gotten so bored... she'd never thought about that before—but she'd have to ask someone for the money. Would Ma give them some if he was the one to ask? Every so often, the boys called out to Ram, whose response was curt, weary. Santee might have told them to let him sit with his thoughts, as she and Ma always had in Bienvenue. She suddenly felt embarrassed for having followed him. Having gone looking for him among the town's embers. Finding herself here, spying on him with his eyes lost in the gorges' outlet, both within reach and inaccessible. He had always refused to be hugged when he was little; he'd fought, slipped under the table, but she'd wanted to hold him. His hair smelled so good and she needed to feel it against her cheeks every so often, she wanted his warmth in the crook of her body, but he could hurt her with a single elbow thrust. He'd bitten her once, then had just gone back to playing, perfectly aware of what he'd done. That's just how he is, Ma said. He's a bit wild. Sometimes she'd lashed out at Ma in exasperation, telling her that Ram was spoiled, that it wouldn't turn out well. Ma always shot back that if she couldn't spoil her only son then who could? And then Santee would flee to her room and cry as Ma yelled from the kitchen that she was the one in trouble. She caught herself crying again here, behind her rock, sobbing so loudly that any of the boys could have heard her. She didn't know where they were, she heard their voices echoing from the ravine's banks: Double-fives, Pass, You're cheating, Wait, who's that over there? One of them whispered, It's Bissoonlall's sister, but quietly so Ram wouldn't get mad at them. The boys with the rocks reappeared. Others who had been fishing were now dragging a huge, reeking eel; their voices disappeared down a path leading to the town. When they sheepishly walked past Ram, he spat—was it because of the stench? He turned to face her determinedly.

She felt exposed, as if naked for the first time, but didn't let it show. He got up and peed against a rock. Then he started looking for his clothes, which he found all over the place. Dressed again in his filthy school uniform, he walked toward her. She crouched behind her rock as she watched him amble over; he was tall, she couldn't see his features, just his dark silhouette rising above the ravine's sides, lost in the murky sky. He strode self-assuredly; she felt somehow detached. She didn't care that he would find her sitting there, haggard, her cheeks wet with tears. Once again. She didn't care that, after looking for him for days on end, it would be he who found her. She stayed put, wringing her hands, looking resigned and resentful. Now that he was before her, safe and sound, she could be as mad at him as she wanted—not for having led her astray from the outset, not for making her roam all over Rose-Hill, but for something unsayable she kept in her heart, something that had been there since she'd been in the cradle that would later hold Ram, something corrosive that nobody had been able to extract. Maybe Pa could have, but he'd passed away before she'd been able to talk to him about it, and even if he had been there, the chance still might never have come. Ma had to have experienced it too, the feeling of living with a wound that never scarred over but not being able to talk about it; Ma had suffered too, but she didn't show it; and Ma, too, hadn't given Santee any chance to talk about her own pain, even though it would have done them good. They could have taken their tea in the kitchen, Ram would have been at school right then, it would have been hot out in Bienvenue, and Ma would have sat down with a sigh, holding her cup and wiping her temples with her odhni, the fields would have been deserted, and there would have been just Ma and her in the little kitchen struggling with their wounds; maybe they wouldn't have needed words or maybe the words would have come to their lips easily, but instead Ma had gone to lie down and sent her to pick up her little brother. It was simply too late, this wound had to be borne within herself, there was no use in grappling with it, since there was nothing that could be done. It didn't need to be like this, though, and there would probably be other wounds, if that could be any consolation, there would probably be other wounds that would make her forget this one. Ram couldn't possibly know any of this as he walked up to her, a stone among the basalt stones of the Grande Rivière.

She and Ram sat on the edge of the rock shelf. He watched the afternoon's colors change along the gorges' crests. Maybe he was watching for some movement in the wild pepper trees that the last of his friends had disturbed. The ravine's sides stopped vibrating, turned gray and calm. Just like his sister's face once her nervous tics had subsided and the creases around her mouth softened.

Every so often he glanced at her: how would this night with her at the bottom of the ravine go, what would happen next... The past didn't matter anymore, didn't have any bearing on his thoughts. Coils of smoke unfurled along the face of the Grand Rivière's cliff, marking an end. Of the dry season, perhaps; if so, they'd be caught by surprise. He could have weathered a flash flood by scrambling up trees and living like the little monkeys who fed on the berries and picnic leftovers by the Tour Blanche. But what about Santee? Her presence changed everything—he couldn't see what he ought to do if the river swelled, someone would have to take care of him now. The other child-monkeys were back safe in their parents' houses, and now that she was here, Ramesh needed to be taken home, too, and she was the only one who could do that.

With each explosion, he jumped. She realized that the town going up in flames, where people were now living in abundance, pushing around overloaded shopping carts, wasn't Ram's but hers, Shakuntala's, and he didn't know this woman. He couldn't brave the smoke rising above the cliff's edge alone, looming over them like a massive night-tree. These thoughts could wait, as patiently as Ram did; she herself, lost in the depths of her wound, was waiting for her sobbing to stop and he, deep in his Grande Rivière ravine as the black tree unfurled over the cliff's ridge, was listening, focusing on her so as not to hear the explosions, watching her hiccups subside under the dark branches, become as regular as a heartbeat.

When she looked up, he was slumped on the rock shelf, his chin pressing into his chest. She stepped around his outstretched limbs, his pale feet wedged into his dirty sneakers. A lock of heavy black hair came down to his thick upper lip, and his chin was covered in a barely visible dark peach fuzz. His breath, which had come to mirror hers, was deep. She climbed along the flat rock to the pool's edge. There was no light to see what was at the water's bottom; clumps of elodea rose up on vines—the last survivors of the drought. A trickle of water from a crack in the lava had traced its path to feed the basin. All the timillions and tilapias and eels crammed into this one space meant a very nice haul for any boy who fished there. She skipped from rock to rock to see the fish that had been so certain the boys wouldn't disturb them anymore slip away. She was happy to be there, alone on the pond's edge while Ram slept. She didn't know the names of the fish or other animals. She wouldn't have wanted someone to tell her, not even if that could mean making up names together. Tadpoles, larvae, the other strange things that fed on slimy algae: they entered her world with their own names—hardly Ramesh's creatures. He was here, sleeping like a baby because she was here. He had handed all the power back to her, but she didn't care about such a gift, she was Shakuntala of the town on fire, of the garden, and of Grande Rivière Nord-Ouest's

critters. Should she ever want to, she could leave
the gorges, choosing to swim in the trickle of water leading toward the sea, changing form at every
twist and turn, mingling with fish and algae. She
wouldn't have to find her way, the water would
take her. She didn't really know whether she was
falling or slipping, she wasn't surprised to feel so
strangely inclined, at the bottom of this ravine no
horizon could be seen, and so there was no hori-
zontal or vertical, there was no sky apart from the
vault of the black tree's branches, and there was
no way of knowing what was beneath the water.

But Princess Shakuntala felt no fear, even
though she had never swum in the river behind
Ma's house. Santee had helped her mother carry
piles of laundry, but never dared stick her feet
in the milky water that the laundresses waded
through unthinkingly, much less strip down on
the sly for a swim while one of the aunties stood
as a lookout. She had fallen into the water one day.
Arms weighed down with a load of laundry that
Ma had just washed, she took the shortcut along
the river. The mud sucked in her flip-flops, and
she remembered the soft mud against her side,
her face, the slow slide into the water. She had
struggled to avoid drowning in water that came

up to other people's knees. Had Ma scolded her, it would have come as a relief. She had soiled an entire heap of white sheets with mud—a scolding and stern slap would have offset the shame she felt amid the scattered clothes in the shallow water as the women, and even Ma, laughed. She'd eventually taken refuge far back from the bank, and Ma had to bring the laundry up to the rocks that Santee refused to ever go past again.

When Ram was woken by a splatter, Santee had disappeared beneath the surface. She hadn't decided to come back up. It wasn't a matter of air but of decisiveness, Shakuntala didn't see the need, it wasn't a question of life or death, there was no line between the two these days. Did she need to undergo a rite of passage by way of these waters, as a puddle creature, did she have to earn this? Ram must have gone through this stage, his childhood was a road paved with gold, he must have done something in a previous life to deserve it… If Ram dove into the water right where some bubbles were still rising, maybe he would be able to help her, but no, she was too big and he wouldn't be able to bring her all the way to the surface. What his presence might do, at least, would be to bring her to her senses. But he didn't do anything; he simply watched the bubbles rise up as if from a spring, the same way he'd watched her cry. It was all the same: while he had been asleep she'd been drowning in her tears, and it wasn't the first time. She needed to come back of her own will; he had lost all the power he once held over this pond where he knew every nook and cranny.

Ram knew he had no way to make his sister decide to resurface in this life—there's no sacrificing yourself by water, only emerging from it, and it would be the water, the obliging water, that bore her back up to him. She was now a creature unfamiliar to him, with his sister's features but put together differently: Ma's cheekbones, like Uncle Vijay's, and Pa's forehead from his passport photo, all these similarities usually ascribed to him at family gatherings, even the thick lips—he couldn't remember Santee's lips, in fact he didn't remember any of her features, just her pout and her slightly forced laugh. When she'd cried the only part of her face not shrouded by her hair had been her nose's blotchy tip. The eyes of this woman drifting in the water were shut, he could look right at her, her hair floated freely around her body tangled in its linen dress; her swaying

arms and legs slowly bore her upward in the ges-
tures not of a drowning woman but of a water
creature with no immediate need for air. Santee
didn't know how to swim, she had often watched
as he horsed around with other children five or six
years old like him while their mother did laundry,
but when they were older they had to tend to the
house and the animals, and were shooed away from
the river by a torrent of curses so they wouldn't
see the women bathing in the nude. He'd never
seen Santee in the water. The woman whose large
nipples and dark crotch stood out against the lin-
en's soaked fibers wasn't covering herself the way
the village women did. She opened her eyes to the
vault framed by the gorges, to the indifferent walls
of the ravine around the rocky shelf, and to him
watching her. The womanly body stood up without much hurry, lumbering with her heavy hips—
her feet must have come across a shoal. Should
we leave now? She furrowed her brow in confu-
sion. Leave? Why? In February's tropical heat the
water was the same temperature as the air. The
water would get cold soon, but today there was
no difference between water and air. It was a matter of leaving this place…leaving… Drought had
stopped the river in its course, all that remained

were this unmoving pond and a thin trickle that might not even reach the valleys of Port-Louis, he'd never followed it with the critters that risked it. Maybe he understood and had stopped with his questions, or maybe he didn't want any crying like in Bienvenue. Maybe he'd given up entirely on trying to convince her to leave.

Footsteps resounded from beyond the river's bend downstream. Restless footfalls. The town loomed large. It was clear to him now he couldn't let her stay here. Halting breaths filled the silent, waiting world, a mad rush scattered stones everywhere. Ram's face hardened—she needed to leave, now. But she lingered, shaded her eyes to make out the newcomer. It was a young man in a khaki uniform whose surefootedness belied his worry. As they watched, he slowed down; usually at this hour there wasn't anyone in the gorges of Grande Rivière Nord-Ouest. His face showed some fear and he steered well clear of them, going up the sparsely vegetated slope to look for a path leading to the clifftop, he slipped, tried again to no avail. The man turned around and looked uneasily at the two in the ravine. Ram pointed out the footpath, and he took it. Where did you come from? she yelled. The man stopped but didn't answer. His eyes flitted from Ram to the woman who had spoken, but he didn't dawdle—the black tree was swelling, blooming overhead. Where did you come from? she repeated. Can't you hear us? Ram turned his back on his sister, discomfited by her presumptuousness. The man nodded his head downstream. He was out of breath and out of words to say what had to be said. The tree was there, that was all the explanation needed. Are there shops down that way? She was dripping; her mud-stained linen dress clung to her skin.

Ram didn't understand who his sister thought she was to be asking the man questions. Women never ventured into the Grande Rivière's gorges; even children who came only did so behind the grown-ups' backs. Ram couldn't even say what exactly it was he'd come here to do, the only water left was in the pond, he didn't like fishing, and he didn't like playing dominoes. The other kids from school liked this place, they called it "the casino" for just that reason, and also to maybe kill a few inedible animals and leave them out to dry in the sun. But the first time he'd followed them, he'd sat on a stone for hours looking up and down the slopes with scattered leaves: Bissoonlall, you coming or what, next time somebody else can be number four if you don't want to play, he'd joined in, the dominoes already set out. After that, he'd started coming here while the others were at school. By himself, just to hang out. The gorges had their own laws, their own tides that he'd come to know. Her intrusion had upended them, and once she was gone, he wouldn't ever return.

The man in uniform, however, was in too much of a hurry to take any interest in her; he went up the path Ram had pointed out, and they could hear the dry grasses rustling for a while longer. Ram would have liked to double back, why not follow the stranger? But that would mean leaving her there, abandoning her at the bottom of the ravine, she wouldn't have let him. He had no choice; he had to wait until she relented. They could have taken a different path, like the one back to the Balfour Garden, they didn't have to follow the young man. They had to get going before night fell rather than continuing toward where the now-fleeing figure had come from.

If he could have read his sister's mind, he'd have known that down there was indeed where she was leading him. He didn't have to retrace his steps, the ravine swallowed him just as the preceding events had. He had to stay fish-like, following rather than fighting the current, as weak as it was. He had to not worry himself sick like Ma who'd spent her life trying to make Pa bring home his paycheck and not drink it away. Then, once Pa was gone, raising Ram. They didn't have long before the day would be gone, just an hour of daylight—her bare feet found the rocks they needed, round enough not to hurt yet steady enough not to roll. Ram trusted her now, had stopped wondering where she'd picked up all this knowledge. He imagined a whole secret life that had gone by unbeknownst to him. To them, rather: he couldn't imagine Ma had any inkling of it. But Ma always knew everything, she had to be in cahoots. He felt exposed, imagining that Ma and maybe even his sister knew all his secrets but hadn't shared any of theirs; they must not have told him anything because he was too little, and fury grew within him, grew each time he stubbed his toe, grew each time he caught sight of his sister's bare feet so nimble on the basalt rocks, grew when he finally saw the red sky of Port-Louis spreading wide over the fires. She, in turn, seemed dazzled or simply dazed. The steep slopes dwindled and they reached the first houses. Ram heard a hubbub in the distance. He couldn't make out the people's words but sensed a crowd. Ram didn't like the thought of so many people, that was what drove him deep into the gorges or into the fields of Bienvenue, someone would always be yelling: Get, Ram, get divan... Ahead were the three bridges of Grande Rivière Nord-Ouest, like triumphal arches welcoming his sister. He didn't understand her hurry; she was now yanking him by the arm. They passed beneath the first bridge. Ram looked up to the deck and beams, high up on the piles that supported the old railroad tracks. He felt ill, wanted to stop. But she went under without even noticing.

Santee is moving toward the sea, she's the water that was missing from the riverbed, her movements flow, and he should do likewise, he shouldn't fight. He tries to match her steps, convinced that she's slowing down. But no, she's practically running, jumping from stone to stone, hiking up her dress with one hand and gripping Ram with the other, a grown-up girl doesn't hold her eleven-year-old brother's hand—her hand feels so soft but she's holding tight so he can keep up with her. She instinctively took his hand beneath the first bridge because the second is as imminent as a wave, a riptide that carries her, she's racing as if she were late to meet someone. But, Santee, nobody's going anywhere, nobody's been waiting for anyone for two days. Old Ma's lost all hope that we'll be back, she's got to have called Uncle Vijay, and made him go to the police, but the police have bigger fish to fry than going to look for two kids who haven't come home because one didn't wait for the other. The police station's on fire, officers are being pelted with stones, nobody's waiting for us, nobody, so...

And then he feels bad; he curses himself for having played hide-and-seek, he can't tell her that in the thickets behind Ma's house, whenever he heard her worried voice several yards away yelling Are you there, Ram, answer me, Ramesh, his heart always pounded as she closed in. Keep looking, try harder, use your brain, and if by some miracle she did find him, it came as a relief. They pass other teenagers, fleeting silhouettes going upriver. They don't even stop, they merge with the darkness, where they're going nobody's ever found again, into deep-rooted memories of long-lost childhood, playing hooky, a sister with long legs and immense, terrified eyes that had missed him by a matter of minutes. No, that's not right, because he would have stayed hidden regardless, he'd have slipped past the teacher at school and out the back door—who's this woman who's found him and is dragging him toward the sea, far below the streets lit by burning buses? They're right there, flipped over right in the middle of the road and blazing in the fire somebody lit, their wheels still flaming circles, women with steel-gray hair, smiling with all their wrinkles, dance all around them. They haven't reached the outskirts of the town, this is a camp in one of the Chamarel forests, they're chanting refrains from seggae songs and their hips swing with a vigor they thought their bodies had lost, a fervor they thought their hearts had forgotten. The teenagers watch them with jealousy, teenagers who don't know what the flames mean.

Sha-kun-ta-la! Sha-kun-ta-la!

Who are those syllables aimed at? Not them, clearly, but the throaty voice from above is good enough for Ram, it's as good as heaven-sent. Let's stop running! They're under the old bridge, the name echoes every which way beneath the arches, but she's still running straight ahead, toward the sea, toward a weak arc of moonlight in the distance. Stop, look, there's someone up there. She hears him, but she thinks it might be a figment of her imagination, or one of Ram's jokes. But no, nobody's joking now. Look, foutou, someone's calling your name! She won't listen, with his whole body he pulls her back, she stops, irritated.

Shakuntala!

Her eyes light up, her neck cranes up to the bridge's beams. What's happening now? He's already regretting having stopped her, it probably would have been better to keep heading toward the sea, to reach it and even drown in it. They can't make out the person up there, who's that little black speck with such a voice? Who's leaning halfway over the railing, yelling Shakuntala? Ramesh sits on a stone as his sister answers. He hears the other one, up above, tell her: Come on up, can you see the path on the bank? Just look, Shakuntala, are you blind or what? Ram doesn't want to take the trail that will lead them up there, he stays put with his eyes fixed on the river's mouth and the little arc of moonlight that his sister has left him. What good is a bit of moonlight on the water going to do him when she's storming the town, when she's going to take it head-on? Ram wants to stay right here on this stone, he wants to lie down in the withered riverbed. He doesn't want to know what's happening up there, he can hear plenty already: people are slinging the sounds of explosions, names, laughter down into the river that will carry them away. He'd prefer for his sister to stay here peacefully with him, for him to be there for her as she cries, for her not to leave him so quickly.

Ramesh!

She's already up there, with that other man, he sees their torsos extending over the railing, the strong wingbeats of their calls. She's above him, perched above his riverbed, her hair will fall around him and he'll play with it, grab hold of it. He'll feel her warm, sweetish breath, and then Ma will come and say: Let your little brother sleep now, it's late, don't keep him up, you can play with him tomorrow. He's going to slip away to the coast, it'll be easy, he just has to take one step toward the arc of moonlight. She shouldn't have left him alone in the riverbed, he'll head down toward the tideway. He has no idea what could be waiting for him there, but he's going to go, and she'll save him before he drowns.

Ramesh! Ramesh! Come along now!

She doesn't want to play. He takes the trail; she's waiting for him up there with a Creole man, Say hello to Ronaldo…why are you sulking? If you don't want to come, just say so, Ronaldo and I can do our own thing. Ram says so and says so again, but to no avail, nobody hears his words. She's talking to the Creole guy, he's telling her something, Where's the Dino-Store warehouse, Ronaldo, why should we bother with the Dino-Store? Ronaldo Milanac points, and she stamps her foot impatiently. It's not close by, though, the man says, it's all the way up by Coromandel. She pouts. Oh, don't be like that, Shakuntala, we've got all night, we'll go nice and slow—the little guy will be able to keep up with us without any trouble, it'll be fun for him. Come on, we can let him see the people breaking into the prison, then we'll take him to the Dino-Store. But she's already gone, so he swallows his thoughts. A few steps and the old stones of the Borstal are already coming into view. The entire road's filled with people gathered in front of the black metal gate, Come on, Ramesh, come on, we're going to miss it all if you don't get a move on… I'm not going to bring you next time, I'll leave you with Ma, you don't want to be left with Ma, do you? So stop it with the whining, we're going to see if we can get to the front. You can't see anything from here, give me your hand, I don't want to lose you again, we're not going to waste the whole night looking for you. I said give me your hand, and she grabs it brusquely just as she herself is being pulled along by Ronaldo. Guys in uniforms are coming down a ladder set against the wall. The crowd shifts and a forklift makes its way through, honking loudly. The driver, a bare-chested teen-ager with a cigarette dangling from his lips and evidently proud to have this job, has driven the commandeered machine out of a garage nearby. Everyone is cheering him on; he waves to the crowd, heads toward the prison, reaches the gate, and maneuvers the forks under it. They know what they're doing, they're all construction work-ers at Makson & Co.—some still have their work overalls on—usually they install automatic gates, not destroy them, and they look downright glee-ful in fact. The forklift groans; the door's a solid one. Finally, rather than give way, it splits in two, from the bottom up it rips just like a canvas sheet, as if the forks were slicing through the metal. Ramesh has never heard steel tear before, it's like the scream of an animal in pain, an execution, and the crowd starts clapping. Rails are inserted to pry apart the two sections of metal—they're go-ing to disembowel the prison. Everybody shoves to get inside. Are we going in? Her eyes gleam. He wants to tell his sister it would be madness; he doesn't want to go into the Borstal, where one of his teachers told him he'd end up if he didn't make more of an effort. He doesn't want to wriggle between those two twisted sheets of metal, you don't just walk into a prison. He's gone past it many times, the entrance faces Royal Road, it's a juvenile detention center. His sister hadn't known that, and suddenly Ramesh doesn't feel too sure of it himself, the freestone building doesn't look like a jail. He sees women coming through the opening with arms full of office supplies, binders and computers, they're having trouble getting through—the metal's razor-sharp. She waits for them to make their way out, then leads them inside. He shudders as he slips between the blades; they could just snap shut, the monster might have been gutted but it isn't dead. Security cameras are still tracking their movements, sweeping frenetically over the inner courtyard with a high-pitched screech. Marauders take them out with well-aimed stones. Teenagers in khaki uniforms emerge from the darkness. Motherly figures are waiting for them, holding babies. There's a pounding on the door of a cell at the far end. She gets closer, dragging her guy along. It's Augustin's cell. Look, it's Augustin's cell. Everybody rushes over. When the lock finally gives way, Augustin steps out into the light.

He's a short man, if he's in the juvenile detention center he can't be twenty yet. But his hair is graying and his features are those of a fifty-year-old man. Outside his cell, he looks at his liberators with all the dignity of a head of state. The others can't stop apologizing for not having freed him sooner. He starts shaking everyone's hands, a woman runs up to him and, sobbing wildly, clutches him. She shrieks his name hysterically. He's too weak to shake her off, a guy pries Augustin from the woman's grip then takes him by the shoulder and waves for the others to follow—they're going to show everyone that Augustin's been freed.

Ram has lost sight of his sister, he only hears: Hurry up, we're going to miss the procession. When he sees her again, she's right beside Augustin, who's bent down to listen to her. Ram gets close. He can't hear what she's telling him, but Augustin responds, Tomorrow in Port-Louis! His smile is triumphant. Ronaldo Milanac comes up to them, he'd been looking for her in the crowd.

He's carrying a computer monitor on his shoulder. Ram wonders what he'll do with it, somebody else must have taken the rest of the computer—there's not enough for everyone. A young woman calls out from far off, asking for someone to bring Augustin to her place, where there's fish curry on the stove. Santee drags Ronaldo and Ramesh into the procession as it moves onto Royal Road, and she tells the Creole: Augustin is that guy who stabbed his sister's lover five years ago, he was in middle school then, everyone knows he did the right thing, his sister's lover was beating her every night, but the court wasn't going to put up with that story, that's how it always goes, and Augustin was put away for fifteen years. They must have forgotten him in the Borstal, but it's all right, he's still young. Ramesh wonders where Santee picked up all this, wants to ask her about it, but Santee's let go of his hand and he's having trouble keeping up with them even though she stops every so often for him to catch up, which forces Milanac to stop as well. She's still holding onto him, telling him things he listens to seriously, things that maybe Augustin had told her.

They follow the procession with less and less interest. Ramesh wants to tell them that they need to get a move on if they don't want to lose track of the leaders—he wants to know where they're going. There aren't as many people around them now, the procession is thinning out, maybe Augustin has reached the woman's house and is eating fish curry, while the rest of them are just ambling at a leisurely pace. Ram is sure that these people were with them at the prison. But where have all the others gone? Where? Neither Santee nor Ronaldo answer him. They're still walking; she's whispering as he listens attentively. On the side of the road is Augustin, sitting on a milestone. He's pulled off the shirt of his khaki uniform because he's hot, and his belly covered in gray hair is dripping. Ramesh would have liked to stop and ask him where everyone else was, and maybe he has other things to say, too, but his sister and her guy aren't paying attention to Augustin. Clearly she knows everything about him, so they leave Augustin on the roadside, lost in his thoughts. Santee is talking, talking, the guy listens; what could she be telling him? He shouts: Where are we going now? She cuts him off: Can't you see I'm talking? She's jabbering about a house: Ma's house isn't worth the hassle of getting to, there's not much to say about the Bienvenue place, it faces the highway and there's an old barn out back. Ram's hungry, nobody's thought about food or drink for ages. They're headed toward the warehouses, there's nothing that way, just the stark outlines of industrial-zone hangars and the raw glare of searchlights. There's definitely nothing to eat. How would you know, you've never been there, she's saying to the guy, telling him about the kitchen. Ma wouldn't have been too pleased if her daughter brought Ronaldo Milanac home; and now Santee's talking about the bed and the armoire. He listens as they walk, walk down streets he doesn't know. No fair, the armoire is Pa's, Ma said I could have it. You don't know what you're talking about. He has to wait for her to stop chattering on. Where did this Ronaldo Milanac come from who's listening to every single thing Santee says? This isn't someone Ma would know; Ma's met with all the nice families that Santee would do well to marry into—nobody has told Ram as much, but he knows, even though these are the sorts of things Ma and Santee never told him.

They have to go down the side of the road to get around a blockade of cars on fire. There's a Toyota, No, that can't be a Toyota, it's a Nissan, But I thought there weren't any of that model, he wants them to stop so they can figure it out. In Bienvenue he'd have known immediately, it would have taken her hours, but here...if only she'd give him a second, it's hard to identify a car that doesn't have a normal shape, there's barely any nickel plating left, and say: Oh, Santee, this one's kogs are gone, look, it doesn't have any left, Santee, did you see? Santee! Santee!

Shakuntala!

She turns around without a word. The cars are all unfamiliar makes that he doesn't recognize, it's too late to tell her, the whole heap has already collapsed. In Bienvenue the owners wouldn't have abandoned their cars, wouldn't leave them to burn like piles of junk. Cars were their pride and joy, and if they got into accidents, they could be found standing next to their dinged cars crying their eyes out and telling their sob stories to any-one who'd listen. These disposable things couldn't be worth a rupee—they just fell apart when they weren't needed anymore and nobody cared.

And besides, nobody needs cars in her town where everybody's on foot, where she never feels tired, where there's plenty of time and people just stroll, and if they run it's not necessarily be-cause there's some rush. It's odd, everyone seems to know each other, they shout out each other's names, tell each other the latest news. There are people asking Ronaldo Milanac where he got the monitor that's on his shoulder, he doesn't answer, he's wary, but she's happy to pipe up: We just came from the prison. The prison? Yes, they set Augustin free. Augustin? Seriously? Yes, he was freed and led a procession away. Augustin was freed, and anyone can go check it out, it's really saying something that they were able to free Augustin. Ramesh wants to chime in, to have his say, especially about Augustin, but he can't get a word in edgewise.

Straight ahead of them is the Dino-Store warehouse. There's no question they've reached their destination. It's clear because Santee and Ronaldo Milanac finally stop. In front of the warehouse is a fiberglass model of a tyrannosaurus, as tall as the three-story-high building it guards. She pulls away from him and gawks at the monster, which Ronaldo Milanac says was a relic of the company's twenty-fifth anniversary celebration. He's talking to Ram because she's not listening. The dinosaur seems to stand a bit stiffly because it was reinforced with an aluminum prosthesis after the unrelenting heat and the weight of its jaw had caused it to start bending over backward. The reptile couldn't have shown up at a better moment—they can catch their breaths, take it all in, and then they'll see about the rest of the night. Ramesh wonders if the easiest thing wouldn't be to go back to the prison even though one of the rules of the game is to never retrace his steps. He can't stop thinking about the riverbed, even though he knows that the night in the sky over the gorges has submerged it in total darkness and the same night here, all around them, is smoldering.

He follows Santee and Ronaldo who have started running toward the warehouse, hand in hand, laughing, as others come out carrying fridges, garden benches, pressure cookers. Wait, wait, he shouts, but his voice is weak now. They've reached the entrance, there's the Dino-Store tyrannosaurus jumping, laughing loudly, encouraging them with its tiny forearms: Hurry up, Don't wait, Everything must go. There are too many people, he tries not to lose track of her long hair, he can't see Ronaldo Milanac anymore, but he knows from the way his sister's running that she's following him. Ram walks, looking all around, trips, and gets overrun by the crowd. Pulls

himself up, he's got to get moving before…before
what, Ram doesn't know. He doesn't see what the
rush is, all he sees is that nobody's laughing anymore, they're all in a frenzy. So he decides he'll
wait for his sister and Ronaldo at the empty end
of the parking lot. He sits right on the asphalt, he
feels better on that harsh surface. If he weren't at
risk of getting trampled, even here where there's
almost nobody, he'd lie down, stretch out all his
limbs, and press his back to the rough ground.
He'd look at the bare sky and his spirit would soar
up in search of the way to Bienvenue. And he has
a feeling that even up there nothing would guide
him, that the conflagrations springing up as vi-
olently as lava flows everywhere to mark Kaya's
death would immediately lead him astray.

Hey there, Shakuntala's brother! comes the
voice of Santee's guy. But what appears is a creature with an oversized head like a dark tadpole's,
staggering across the Dino-Store parking lot.
Ram gets up. It's Ronaldo Milanac blindly lurch-
ing forward, carrying a huge, padded armchair,
a massive piece of furniture, and his entire upper half is hidden between the armrests. It's like
he's trying to fight off a hulking monster set on
chomping down on his head and chest. If Ram

hadn't been sitting on the ground, Ronaldo never would have seen him. Where's my sister? In the Dino, Ronaldo barks out. He bends over double, unloading his burden, and pulls himself away. His T-shirt is torn and his face is bruised. Ramesh imagines that he's narrowly escaped a nasty end in the armchair's belly. Ronaldo Milanac's won this fight and laid his prize before Ramesh like an offering. It's an odd gift, Ramesh would have liked something else, like a mountain bike. He's seen a few going past still in their plastic wrapping, but of course the best things have disappeared the fastest. Ram should acknowledge the sign of respect, Ronaldo Milanac has been perfectly nice this whole time and he carried the armchair so Ram wouldn't be uncomfortable, he must have forgotten that he said earlier that they'd go nice and slow and they still haven't found anything to eat or drink. Watch this until we come back, will you? Okay, Shakuntala's little brother? Ramesh says yes automatically, but he's not just somebody's little brother, especially not when Santee's lost her head and decided to go prancing around in the Dino-Store. He's Ram, but come to think of it he's not so sure about that. Some sort of transformation happened at some point and he actually might not be the same anymore. Shakuntala wants you to wait there, right where you are. Don't go running off without giving us a heads-up again. Just be good and sit in this armchair, that's not so hard, right? Sit your ass in there and I'll bring over some other things from Shakuntala for you to watch. Watch? Yeah, would it kill you to help? Seriously, keep your eyes open so nobody nicks them. You know, this Dino-Store stuff is worth real money. Watch this chair, it's pleather, you got any idea how much that would cost over in Rose-Hill? Ramesh doesn't understand why his sister is looking for furniture, what's in Bienvenue is good enough, Ma bought some new stuff not that long ago, although that furniture wasn't as impressive as this. And where would this even fit in Ma's place? Okay, good, I'm going now, Shakuntala's waiting for me. Ronaldo Milanac wipes away a trickle of blood from a gash below his eye. Just don't move, or your sister's going to give me an earful, you hear me? Ramesh watches him head back so Shakuntala won't get mad. Why hadn't his sister come herself? Why is she asking this guy to do things for her? Ramesh puts his hand on the chair's back unthinkingly—it's a rather tall Executive, the fabric is a nice texture, soft to the touch. The armrests could swell up like cows' udders, Ramesh can see why it was so hard for Ronaldo Milanac to pull himself free. He can't really see anyone stealing it; it's a very heavy chair and he wonders where Milanac found the strength to lug it all the way out to the parking lot. It must have been one of the labors Ronaldo undertook to win his sister's love.

Why aren't you sitting in it, you gogot? This time Ronaldo is furious. He's back, towering over Ram, dripping with sweat and blood, his shirt gone and his body covered in bruises. He's survived the second tussle. I'm working my ass off and I tell you what to do, but you can't be bothered to do it? What's wrong with your head? I think Shakuntala was right not to trust you, you don't care. Ramesh flinches at those words. He decides Ronaldo Milanac has to be exaggerating. Santee couldn't have said something like that, she ought to be here to set this man straight. This time, Ronaldo's brought back a mahogany table with carved legs like a giant octopus's tentacles. He's so exhausted that he throws it on the asphalt rather than setting it down. The table lands with a dull thud. Ram is perched on the armchair... What about the table? If you're on the chair, what are you going to tell Shakuntala if the table gets stolen? That you were just catching a quick nap? You think she'll buy that? Some other men walk past, carrying an armoire with its doors swinging back and forth, squeaking with every step. You sons of bitches, don't you think for a second that you can make off with our chair or table, we want them both, get it? Get a move on, then, go grab yourself a bed too, they snickered. And don't forget your girl if you give two shits about her.

You think it's funny to fight over furniture and then see it all get stolen? Ram doesn't know what to say so Ronaldo will trust him. Suddenly, the man makes up his mind: I've got it, I'll put the chair on the table, it'll be safer, and if one of those thugs comes back, you yell, or at least hold them off, I don't care as long as you don't just lie there dead as a mummy. With a forceful grunt, Ronaldo Milanac lifts the chair and sets it on the table. Your turn now, and he grabs Ramesh under the arms to put him on the table, but it's a struggle, he doesn't really have it in him anymore, he's worked so hard to make Shakuntala happy, All right now, no excuses, you're going to stay put right there, I've got more to do. Ramesh doesn't have a choice, so he sinks into the chair with its soft new upholstery. This wouldn't be such a bad way to go: he'd lose consciousness before he felt the chair's jaws closing on him, and once it had digested him, he'd climb down from the table and crawl away. He can just hear Ronaldo's voice: I'm going back to Shakuntala, she's found us a sleigh bed, I don't know how I'm hauling it out, but she won't be happy with anything else, even if she has to stay there forever so those idiots don't take it. I'm going to go see Shakuntala, she's waiting for me, I'm coming back... His words fade as he runs, the tyrannosaurus bows down to the hero heading into his third labor. Ronaldo Milanac has an iron will. A gust of heat buffets Ram's cheeks, glimmers flicker over the dinosaur's scales. Sitting in his chair atop the table in the middle of the parking lot, Ram watches people going past. Everyone in the lot can see him, some people look up at him fearfully, this time, there's no risk he'll get trampled. He'd like this parking lot better if it were empty—people are running and yelling that the police are coming, but there aren't any riot squads or firemen, just the tyrannosaurus plunging slowly toward the asphalt. Ram wonders what Ronaldo Milanac and his sister are doing, it'd be nice if he were with them, maybe he'd come across them in a big bed under rumpled sheets, having made their peace with the armoire being stolen already, and maybe even the chair and table that they'd entrusted to him. They might be asleep. But Ramesh can't go, the chair's got him trapped among the bunches of grapes sculpted in the mahogany of its arms, it's rocking him so that he'll fall asleep like the dinosaur. His sister does have good taste in furniture, even if Ma's so practical that she'll turn down the table with carved legs strong enough to support an armchair.

And even if he didn't find them, if they'd fled with the others through a rear door, although he hasn't seen any other doors, the one thing he'd definitely find would be the abandoned sleigh bed with rumpled sheets burned by the first sparks and them nowhere and some people, the last ones, pushing and shoving with their arms full of Valentine's Day teddy bears and plastic Christmas trees, Get out of the way you idiot, beat it, I swear to you, and one of them would slap him so he'd get a move on, There's no time to explain, or just because he's not Creole, but that can't be what happens, What are they up to in there, Where'd they come from, Where'd the other one go who ended up here with the Black guy in the huge bed that everybody wanted, getting so hot and heavy with that two-faced bastard that they forget about him sitting outside, reigning over the empty parking lot from his armchair throne on the table while everybody's running and yelling, they've all smelled smoke and where there's smoke…everybody knows, what's the point of explaining in these days when there's nothing to do but run, there's only one door, the front entrance, she'll be with Ronaldo Milanac, he wouldn't have left her to protect the big bed all by herself after completing the first two labors. All by herself. No, he wouldn't have abandoned her. Ram hasn't seen Ronaldo come out. Even from within the armchair's clutches, Ram would have seen, Ram would have known. Maybe they cleared out, maybe they haven't even turned back to look for him or warn him, it's hard for him to be sure, but deep down he's sure, he's absolutely sure, he has to accept it, but he'll never be able to say it to the police who'll never come or will come too late, he doesn't have the words to describe these wild days with so much fire, so he'll say whatever to anyone who asks, investigation after investigation, he'll parrot back whatever they say.

As for Ma, he won't tell her a thing either.

He won't have the time to, because she'll leave straightaway, she won't even ask him, Where's your sister? She's never asked him that. She's always asking Santee about him, and he resents her for that. But both of the women are gone now, and he's stuck in the armchair atop the table, everyone can see he's all alone. He has a feeling the policemen are going to lock him up with the others, they have to be up to something, No, of course this kiddo doesn't have to be thrown in with the others, Sure he does, doesn't matter how young they are, when they're raised in the cité, even the littlest ones know how to steal and start fires and throw stones or Molotov cocktails, Can't you see he's not even Creole, Creole or not, who knows how many nights he's been out, listening to the older guys brag about fires, break-ins, looting, they have to be up to something, Ram is sure of it, he'll play along, but why haven't Santee and Ma come to find him yet, nobody's coming.

**CARL DE SOUZA** is a writer born and living in Mauritius. He graduated with degrees in biology and math from the University of London before pursuing a career in education at various levels. He has led an intense sports life, mainly in badminton, which is the background of one of his novels. He has published short stories and six novels in France, of which *Kaya Days* is his first to be translated into English.

**JEFFREY ZUCKERMAN** lives and works in New York City. After a degree in English from Yale University, he became a translator from French of authors ranging from Ananda Devi and Shenaz Patel to Jean Genet and Hervé Guibert. He has been a finalist for the TA First Translation Prize and the French-American Foundation Translation Prize, and has been awarded a PEN/ Heim translation grant and the French Voices Grand Prize.

## TRANSLATOR'S NOTE

*My thanks to Ariel Saramandi and Khatleen Minerve, without whose bagaz ek duser this translation would not have had half its kouler.*

*And to Carl de Souza—for his amiability, his open welcome to Mauritius, and this liv etonan.*